YOUNG

IN THE AGE OF CHAMPIONS

DENELDA BENDSEN

YOUNG — In the Age of Champions

ISBN print: 978-1-7773717-0-8

ISBN ebook: 978-1-7773717-3-9

www.denelda.bendsens.com

This is a work of fiction. Names, characters, places and incidents are the product of the author's imagination or used fictitiously, and any resemblance to actual persons, living or dead, business establishments, events or locales is entirely coincidental. Or deliberately on purpose, depending on how well the author likes those about whom she is writing.

Cover art by Cscreatives

ACKNOWLEDGMENTS

To my husband, Poul Bendsen, I offer the most heartfelt thanks for your love, support and encouragement. Your helpful suggestions have improved the quality and made it fun to write.

For offering insights and experiences on publishing, grammar, grieving, Seattle culture and disgust with the aging process, I thank Dianne Gillespie, Tamara Paulin, Susan Jamison, Patricia Sparks, Patricia Tuton, and Kate Zeiller.

To my writer's group, WIP, thanks for your support, retreats and safe space for each writer in progress.

To my editor, Megan Records, whose young eyes and fearless criticism pointed out countless areas for revision, thanks a lot!

Cally at Cscreatives, thanks for your patience and continued positive attitude as the work progressed on my covers.

Formatting is thanks to Jacqui Nelson — a task I'd rather not tackle.

For inspiring this trilogy, I thank David A Sinclair, PhD. His revolutionary research on aging has changed the way I live and look at life.

CHAPTER 1

Torn with loss, thoughts cloud with grief.
My partner, gone! There's no relief.
My few left years promise pain —
Love gone, my tears will now remain.

The heart monitor tone pierces the silence as Ben's mottled blue-purple hand grows cold in mine. His pale face peaceful, released from years of cancer's pain and anxiety. Instead of the vibrant masculine figure who was my husband, here lies an old man who might have been his father.

His death is not the end of my story. It is the beginning. After forty-two years of a wonderful marriage, losing my best friend leaves me devastated. The last three years were tough while Ben transformed, slipping away. I transformed too. Like my backyard trees stripped bare by October storms can't imagine leaves, blossoms, and fruit of a future season, I am numb to the possibility of any joy. His life is over. I may never be alive again.

Nurses bustle around, moving me back to a chair against

the beige wall while they deal with machines and what remains of the man I love. This chair is where I have waited for many days, watching Ben drift in and out of consciousness. He had stopped eating and drinking. We knew the end was near. I close my eyes as tears slip down my cheeks.

* * *

The physical pain of losing my partner is constant. I drag through our updated Craftsman house on Capitol Hill in Seattle, Washington. Here we raised our children the best we could. Our home, close to downtown and everything we loved to do, is empty as am I. After the cremation, this is where I hold the wake. Darlene and Gord, with successful careers and marriages, travel to honor their father and are comforted by their spouses. They will think of Ben with sadness, but I am ripped apart. My husband was always there for me during our marriage. His illness consumed me, and now his absence reminds me of my loss.

"Take care of yourself, Mom," says Gord, his brawny arms affectionate in his embrace. Carefree and spontaneous, his life with a playful Aussie nurse seems to suit him.

"Call if you need anything. We are only a few hours away," says Darlene, her arms crossed over her tummy. When I release Gord, she gives me a brief hug and they leave together with their partners, catching up on the years since they have been kids in Seattle.

At the gathering at our, or should I say "my" house, I hold it together. Besides our kids, many people who loved Ben come to wish me well. Ben's friend Harvey lingers after most have gone.

"I'm sorry for your loss, Jeni," he says taking my hand. "I know what you're going through."

"It's good of you to come, Harv. Where's Iris?" I look up, my expression blank.

"Iris passed away. That's why I haven't been around for a while." His eyes glaze with tears. "My loss absorbed me. I didn't see anyone until today. I thought you could use a friend." He is still holding my hand.

"I'm sorry. You're right about being hung up on one's own grief. I knew Iris was ill but, with Ben's situation, I never thought to reach out. If I can do anything, you know where I am. I won't be out too much either." I walk him to the door where we hug.

Iris and Harvey were among our closest friends for years. Renting a forty-foot Tully Craft and cruising the San Juan Islands with them provided some of our best memories. We were carefree and relaxed together and always came home refreshed. Our children loved the front bunk where they played forever with dinky toys and Barbies. At night Ben and I slept there while Harv and Iris made the lounge sofa into a pull-out bed. The kids had sleeping bags in the wheelhouse and on cloudless nights we left the cover off. They could imagine being astronauts travelling the universe. We found coves with water warm for swimming, schools of salmon eager to grab hold of our lures, and anchorage where we would cook the fillets on the grill. I swear I'd put on five pounds every time we were with them. We were constantly eating together. Picnics, barbecues, house parties — all included more food and drink than we needed. When their only daughter went off to college, they downsized to a condo in Kirkland. We've seen less of them since retirement as they spent their free time traveling the globe. Now Iris is dead, and so is Ben. I shudder at the thought. Growing old sucks, big time! I bite my lip until it throbs like my pulse.

"That's the last of them," says Carol, closing the door on neighbors who wanted to stay and clean up.

The cheerful, stocky woman has been my friend since high school where we played on most of the school teams together. Even though she is still fun, she left athletics behind in her teens. When we won the city high school badminton doubles title, I played deep while she dashed at the net. She was the point guard I fed on fast breaks in basketball. I'd rip down the rebound, take one dribble to the sideline, and, with her sprinting over center-line, I'd hit her in time for a lay-up. As a back-up setter, she shared the championship trophy for high school volleyball. Carol was skilled at track while I took care of the field events: javelin, high jump, discus, shot put, and even long jump. She was the manager for the swim team where I loved freestyle and backstroke. I could never imagine my life without sports. It is fundamental to who I am.

Ben loved that my passion for sport kept me fit and healthy. He encouraged competitions in Masters and Seniors Tournaments locally and in other states. When my non-athletic husband couldn't travel to tournaments, my teammates offered camaraderie. For the past three years, my first concern has been Ben. I haven't been to the gym or on any sports' trips. I miss being an athlete.

Carol's dark brown eyes, which twinkle with mischief, now show concern. Her beauty and young marriage didn't last. Her school grades were good, but she dropped out of college and settled for many unskilled jobs over the years. Her talent was getting us into trouble and making it seem to be my idea; now, she knows what I need. We've always been best friends, but my marriage tore us apart. I think this often happens when wives give their husbands priority over friendships. Since his cancer diagnosis, here she is — back to help. I can't imagine life now without Carol. The sight of her scurrying around doing the clean-up fills me with warmth. I force a smile as my eyes betray my inner pain.

She takes the plates I have gathered from the living room tables and sets them down. I throw my arms around her and sob. She's a lot shorter than me. And even though we might look ridiculous, that hug — my best friend's embrace — is what I need at this moment. I love that she smells like gardenias. She holds me for a long time before we step back. I swallow the sob I am holding. We nod, our eyes locked in agreement, and finish clearing up.

Carol lightens the mood. "Who was that handsome man holding your hand a few minutes ago?"

"Ben's friend Harvey. Can you believe his wife passed away, and I have been so caught up in my personal pity I never even knew she died? I knew she was ill and never checked on her. I'm a lousy friend. I hope he can forgive me."

"Oh, it looked like he has forgiven you, Sweetie. Soon for asking you out though,"

"Anytime is too soon to ask me out. I never want to love another man. I want Ben back." I wipe my face with the tee-towel which hangs on the front of my oven.

"You will get through this. Life will be better than ever," she says as she hugs me before grabbing her coat off the hook by the door. "We'll figure out what your future will be like."

Her last words before leaving me alone are a distant buzz echoing in my brain. Figure out my future! I am at the grim end of a tunnel with a barely visible twinkle of light in the distance. Shivers from the icy walls encourage a tiny step forward.

Without thinking, I lock the door behind her. The room,

empty of her energy, fills with Ben's absence. I slump over the pain in my chest. Dragging from room to room, I turn off all the lights and trudge upstairs.

I'm sitting on our bed, staring at the closet full of Ben's clothes. What happens to me now? Almost seventy, my clothes are comfortable and shoes sensible. I've disposed of all negative acquaintances. Nothing sexy hangs in my closet. That's what seventy is like, right? Wait for the chronic illness of aging to become infested, its subtle tentacles creeping into my unsuspecting body. Or maybe into my mind. Dementia, stroke, heart disease, cancer — all possibilities. We can't even choose our fate. I rock back and forth as I weep aloud — afraid, angry and bereft.

In the modern bathroom beside the walk-in closet, my electric toothbrush hums while I open the medicine cabinet and see his aftershave. For minutes I stand there smelling his hairbrush, fresh and masculine, tooth paste dribbling into the sink. I miss him so much. My mouth tastes like dusty garlic wrappings. It will take more than swirling minty mouthwash to improve it. My skin has the texture of dry crinkled paper — and my hair — the mirror isn't my friend today.

I can't believe he's gone.

Could he be out of town and come home to open the door any minute? Even last month while Ben was in hospice, I had a purpose. Maintaining a cheerful face, I visited every day and kept his friends updated on his progress. Thanks to the internet and group contact details, one daily note informed dozens of his close friends. Many of them visited him until last week and daily I would get acknowledgements, consolations, and thanks for keeping them in the loop. Now I just hurt.

* * *

For days, I stop as waves of grief wash over me. I am alone, vulnerable, afraid, sad, angry, and even guilty for being alive. During the next month, countless tasks consume me: writing letters, phone calls, dealing with Ben's estate and investments, erasing his life from mine. How can God punish me by taking the man who was everything to me? He was such an incredible person, the one people would seek to solve a problem, to share splendid news, or to ask for advice, and yet that didn't save him! He was my joy.

My only pleasure lately is eating the casseroles that friends drop off — and it shows. My baggy top hangs loosely over the elastic band of my sweatpants, concealing a bulge of fat riding above. I grab a handful on each side of my belly in disgust. Hardly a person worthy of the trophies stashed in my closet. For one chapter I was an athlete — competing for my school, my city, my state, and even my country. That is in the past. Sure, I continued to compete in senior volleyball until Ben's health declined. I miss my sports, my children, and my job in the pharmacy. Sliding to the floor, my back to a corner, I hug my knees and search for purpose. Now, the chapter where I'm a loving wife — it's over too. All the things I have loved are dead to me. I might as well close the book. This last chapter is not worth living. But there is still Carol.

* * *

She bursts through the door using the spare key on one of her frequent visits. I can hear her bounding up the stairs.

"Hi Bud. How's it going today?" She throws open the

drapes above my bed. I peer from under my pillow. I'm not ready to face the day — any day.

"I can't Carol. I can't get rid of Ben's things. I don't want him to go," I sob.

"I know it's hard. Keeping his clothes won't bring him back, Honey. Let me help," she says. "Why don't you keep a few of his things, a sweater or jacket; I'll take the rest to the Thrift Store. There are people who need these clothes." Standing in the closet's door, she pulls a handful of hangers off the left rack.

"Can you leave me in bed while you do that?" I ask.

"No, splash some water on your face and throw on some clothes. We need some sorting boxes or bags," she says. "I could use some lunch and you haven't had breakfast. Why don't you rustle something up?"

I take some deep breaths until I'm strong enough to raise my head. The storage bins are in the basement. These jeans I wore yesterday are fine and this shirt still smells okay. What do I have in the kitchen? I'm exhausted. Thank goodness Carol has energy because I'm drained.

"Carol, are bran flakes and muffins okay? That's all I've got," I say as she stands in the door with the first bin of clothes. Ben's Bin, the first of Ben's Bins. How many will there be?

"Do you have more storage boxes?" Carol asks. "Bran flakes are fine. How old are these muffins?"

"They're okay. I'll pop them in the microwave," I say, setting cutlery on the counter where we can pull up stools.

"I appreciate your help, Carol. Can you sort his tools next? Maybe you can sell some of them," I say.

"No rush with the basement stuff. But sure, after I finish the clothes. I need another box for upstairs."

Onto the stool, I drag with the warmed muffins and pour

milk into my bowl of cereal. Eating seems to be the right thing. Why didn't I think of that? If Carol hadn't come, I would stay in bed all day. It's been a month since the funeral, and I have not been out except to deliver Ben's legal papers for the attorney. What would I do without my best friend? Carol washes up the dishes and leaves them in the tray.

"I'll drop these two bins at the thrift store and get the charitable donation receipt for your taxes. You get to write these off against your income," she says on her way out. "Ever done your own taxes?"

"Ben did them, or he had the accountant do them, I don't know," I say. For the past years I have taken over tasks for Ben if he wasn't able. I have become very competent in many areas out of necessity. But now I am struck, at a physical level, by the realization that I am responsible for everything. We have depleted our personal accounts with the years of hospital bills. Insurance pays the major portion of the expense of health care, but there have been thousands out of our pocket every month. My stomach churns and the room swims around me. I make it upstairs and crash on the unmade bed, sobbing.

CHAPTER 2

My pit so deep, my world so bleak.
"Believe in yourself," I hear her speak.
On her shoulders, I climb 'til a glimmer of light
Points to the future, out of the night.

I can't get through this myself. In the mirror I see an old woman, though only sixty-nine. When did this happen? When did I get this muffin-top over my jeans? I grab rolls of fat above my waist, soft and jelly-like. My brow furrows as I shake my head in disgust. I move closer to my image, parting my hair where the blond ends meet the salt and pepper roots. When did my hair gray? There are age spots on my face. I haven't noticed these before. I rub a large one on my temple. Yup, an age spot! I ache from arthritis. My energy is low. It is an effort to climb the stairs or make the bed.

Sighing a deep breath, I back into the wall, an old habit instilled by my mother to ensure that her tall children never slumped. While I was at university, my older brother died in a car accident. At least Ben made it to seventy-three. My shoulders cave forward and my chin drops toward my chest. Instinctively, I straighten, forcing my shoulders to touch the wallpaper, and my head lines up with my spine. Whoa, way back there! Even that is better. Thanks, Mom. I can breathe freely.

My parents passed away a few years back. But, like straightening against the wall, many memories warm me. I want to think about Ben with love and joy, not anger and sadness. A vision forms. I see through the distortion for the first time. I'm not giving up. I want to live again. There is a thick layer of dust on my tall chest of drawers. Have I become an old, fat, frumpy, lousy housekeeper? A sock found lying by my bed, swishes clean every surface, and gets tossed into the hamper with errant items scattering the room.

What am I going to do now? My posture isn't the only thing that needs fixing. Conscious of the tension between my shoulders, several slow, deep breaths help relax me. I try to wrap my head around my depression, gaining a little control of my frame of mind. I have work to do to make myself into someone I can love.

I'm an athlete; perhaps I need a coach. For over sixty years, team sports have been part of my life. Athletics have taught me to organize my time, to focus, to cope in stressful situations. They have been more than a hobby and an outlet for my competitive nature. Basketball was my primary passion, but after the age of fifty, I replaced it with volley-ball. Both are team sports and very physical, but my aggressiveness on the court was less apt to cause injuries if there was a net between me and my opponent. My success in sports gave me self-esteem. Boy, self-esteem is something I could use right now! A coach could devise a plan to help me get through this depression — to restore joy and purpose.

Little by little, warmth creeps back into my body. I straighten again, with chin raised; a glimmer of hope quickens my step.

My pulled bedroom drapes invite the welcoming blue sky and sunshine into my gray life. A branch, in need of pruning, dances shadows over my spread and, as I watch, a perched wren peers in, singing her delicate tune. It's rare to hear them this time of year.

* * *

With Carol's help, I schedule an appointment at the Life Coaching Institute in Bellevue. As the sun settles into the western skyline, I park in front of a modern one-level building. My black leather boots kick at colored leaves on the path to the front door. The air smells fresh. I've dressed for the first time in months. My long blonde hair ties in a messy bun. In gray slacks with a violet leather jacket topping a crisp white blouse, I don't look like I weigh almost two hundred pounds. People always say, "You're tall. You can carry your weight." That's a polite way of saying, "You're huge — tall and fat." But today I look professional. I mean business!

This is significant for me. I'm excited to start a new chapter. Ben's wife will become her own person, whatever that means. Knots in my chest show this is the start of either an important competition or a life-changing event. It's not a game, so I guess it's the latter.

Inside, I settle on one of the two stylish, orange leather and chrome chairs. A chocolate brown turtleneck hugs Beverly, a scrawny woman in her mid-forties, sitting across from me behind a modern teak desk. Black frames display qualification certificates illegible on the wall behind her.

"We do most of our coaching in phone meetings," she explains. "I rarely work face to face. It requires a three-month contract, but this introductory meeting is free."

"Beverly, I want to move on after my husband's death. Joy and purpose have disappeared. I need a plan for my future," I say.

"What do you intend your plan will do?" she asks, leaning forward in her swivel chair but maintaining eye contact with a professional air of concern.

"It will get me back in shape. I'll have more energy and strength. I want a life filled with joy. Right now I'm depressed, fatigued, and lack purpose," I reply.

"Tell me more about your plan." Is it her perfume or the vase of flowers perched beside her computer which wafts a gentle fragrance my way? Does she have a fellow who sends flowers, or does she get them for herself at the market? Focus Jeni.

She seems to know what questions will get to the heart of my problem. I ponder my answer. "I want to have a strong, healthy body so I don't end up following Ben to the grave. I want to become fit, energetic and attractive again. Not for someone else. I want to like my reflection." I can buy myself flowers too.

"Do you know how?" asks Beverly.

"Yes. Exercise, low carbs, lots of water." I surprise myself. If I've known this all this time, why haven't I been doing it? Did I need a coach to remind me?

"What else would you change in your life?"

I need a purpose. "I've always loved to play volleyball, and I used to compete in age-division tournaments before Ben's illness. So, I'll get back into these as soon as I'm fit. This might give me purpose. Right now, I am useless."

"Do you want more than being fit and getting back to

your games?"

After a moment of silence, I continue, "I want the years back which have sucked the life out of me. I want to be young again. I want that drive where I can take on the world. I want to contribute to society again. Can I do that?"

"With my help, you will achieve most of these goals. I will support you every step of the way. We'll set up a three-month contract where I will hold you accountable by phone each week. It is an effective way of making life changes." She pauses as if to be sure she has my attention. "Getting back the past years is impossible. With the help I offer, we can do everything else," she says. A subtle smile creeps over her face. She is laughing at the possibility of becoming young again.

Why would I need more meetings when I can do all I mentioned with Carol's help? I'm sure we can get me in shape and back to sports. I want to turn back the clock. I want more than being a fit old lady playing some sad excuse for volleyball. But first things first, I guess.

Is this meeting a waste of time? No, it helps me form the steps to move forward. As the sports coach instills direction without being involved in the exercise, her mere presence causes focus and improvement in her athletes. Players could show up at the gym and workout. They know how to do it already; but when the coach is present, much more gets accomplished.

Beverly smiles. She thinks I'm one of her usual clients who needs their hand held. But I'm a help-me-see-the-vision and get-out-of-my-way type of woman. A vision. That's all I need.

"Thanks for meeting with me, Beverly. If I need more sessions, I'll be happy to sign up," I say standing and extending my hand. I float out of her office and back to my car. It's hard to keep to the speed limit; I'm high on the ideas storming within me. I'm slowed by Seattle's insane afternoon traffic as I take the on-ramp to I-405. My mind races, but my foot hardly touches the gas. I will get in shape with strength and energy to compete again. This will be difficult, considering how run down I've become. But Beverly showed no hope for gaining the years back. Why would I go back to her unless she had some secret solutions? The rest we can do ourselves.

* * *

Carol meets me for lunch at the deli near my home.

"You've helped me with everything since Ben's death. It's a comfort having you near. I could never have cleared Ben's things without you. There is something else I need help with," I say reading the wall menu as we stand in the entrance.

She turns with a serious look. "Whatever you need. You know I'm here for you."

"I hate the way I am — frumpy and discouraged. I am weak and lack energy. I plan to change all that and become fit again. That session with Beverly wasn't perfect. She says I can't get the years back that I lost looking after Ben, but I'm not giving up. Will you help?" She nods. "Will you join me to work out every day?"

She can tell I will do this and won't want to miss out. After a pause she says, "I'll commit to five days a week. Does that work?" Gazing down, self-conscious of her size sixteen girth, "It wouldn't hurt for me to work out," she mumbles.

"And I will start eating healthy. Will you help me get rid of all the carbs: potatoes, bread, rice, and pasta? We can drop it at the food bank or throw it out. I don't care."

She digs in her bag for her wallet. "Okay if I take some home with me? I'll be your support, but that doesn't mean I will do your diet."

A salad for me, Carol devours a BLT at a small table by the window. She could use this make-over too, but not for me to suggest. I love her the way she is, but I think she would be healthier if she made some changes too. Forget it, Jeni. She seems happy with her life the way it is. My depression lessens as I fill with hope and optimism. This is the right direction for me.

"At three this afternoon, I'll pick you up. I'm buying memberships at Rival Fitness so we can go as often as we like," I say as we leave the deli.

"You don't have to do that. I can afford my own," she says, walking toward her red Mazda.

"Even though you can, you're joining with me. I'm doing it for me, not for you," I say unlocking the car next to hers. While I'm focused on getting in shape, this is one expense that's not negotiable.

"Fair enough. I'm doing it for you, not for me," she laughs, pouring herself into her driver's seat.

Included with the cost of memberships is a trainer for one hour to orient us, make a personal workout plan, and teach us to use the equipment. He's young and muscular. With each exercise he encourages and laughs, placing his hands on our bodies as he straightens our techniques. I think Carol makes mistakes so he will come and touch her. She knows how to do all these exercises already. We both worked out when we played team sports years ago. She has fine weight lifting form. I smile and wink at her, and her saucy grin proves I am right.

Near the end of our first session, while doing our free weights on the benches at the far end of the gym, someone catches my eye. An attractive woman dressed in florescent green and black spandex climbs onto a stationary bike near the edge of a long row of exercise machines. She looks familiar: red curly hair, round cheeks, and a-turned-up nose.

"Hey Carol, doesn't that red-head on the bike look like Dorothy Adams from Garfield High?"

"Damn right. Maybe it's her daughter. Dot's seventy, but this woman is fifty tops,"

"I've finished here. I will go find out," I say.

Removing her headphones when I approach, a big smile stretches from ear to ear. "Hi Jeni," the cyclist says. "I haven't seen you for maybe twenty years."

"I thought it was you, Dot. You look amazing. I'm here with Carol. Does working out keep you looking this young?" I say, loosening my tee-shirt over my tummy, embarrassed by my appearance.

"Well, there's more to it than just exercise, I've found," she says, slowing the machine and stepping off. "Want to get a drink in the lounge?"

"Go ahead. I'll grab Carol and join you."

Carol picks up her towel, wipes her face, and says, "Her daughter?"

"No, it's Dot. Let's have a drink with her in the lounge,"

Carol's jaw drops in amazement. "What does she know we don't?"

Having finished our first workout, with our jackets retrieved from wall hooks, we join Dorothy in the lounge. "Hey Dot, how you bin?" asks Carol.

"I'm doing great. I see you've joined Rival. I've been here almost three years. Don't you love Billy? He's the trainer who showed you around," Dot says, filling her cup from the upside-down bottle of icy water.

"Yeah, he's adorable." I look at Carol, whose eyebrows raise as she nods with enthusiasm. "You said there's more to your youthful appearance than exercise. What do you mean?" If there is more to my make-over plan, I need to know. I want the same results she has! I know lots of people who have eaten smart and exercised, but have not seen serious changes.

"I've lost forty pounds, but not only by exercising. I changed the way I eat," she says, freeing her red mane from a headband and sipping from her water bottle.

I agree, "I'm purging my house of carbohydrates. I'm eating salads from now on,"

"Yeah, carbs get cut way back, but I'm eating Keto — high fats — no carbs," Dot says.

"I've heard of Keto. It's quite a fad," says Carol.

"It's not a fad for me," Dot says. "I can't imagine eating any other way. The high-fat content lets me fast intermittently without being hungry. That has helped with weight loss and high energy."

Keto and intermittent fasting. I must Google when I get home. It looks like it works for her. She was in my senior year Biology class, where we competed for the highest marks. She was pretty, popular and smart. I guess I was smart and skilled at sports too. Carol and I didn't have time to worry about the popular crowd. Cheerleaders went to every boy's game but only showed up if we made state finals. Unlike most, Dot was friendly, despite not seeing us at the exclusive parties of the popular crowd. Last time I saw her was at our twentieth reunion, I think. She looked like the rest of us then. Whatever she's doing, it's working for her.

"Dot, it's great bumping into you today. I'm making some major changes in my life. You are an inspiration! Do you come here every afternoon?" I put on my jacket, preparing to leave.

"About three days a week, three to four o'clock lets me finish before the after-work crowd comes in," she says. "I have more to tell you, but that's enough for now. Good luck."

"Okay, we have work to do," I say, my mind racing, but Carol looks puzzled. We haven't discussed this yet, but I'm bursting to get the details cemented into a vision.

As we walk, I say, "I will research Keto and fasting. I'll have my plan in place by our workout tomorrow."

"I'm sure you will," she chuckles. "I'm on board to help you do whatever you want, but don't expect me to follow your hare-brained scheme. There are many diets and lifestyles — cleanses, fasting, supplements — they'll drive you crazy. They're based on anecdotal evidence, nothing to prove they work. You get all enthusiastic; then you fail. I know. Look at me. I've been there. I diet for a week, fall off the wagon, get down on myself, comfort-eat until I find a new diet. Just saying. I think you are amazing the way you are. It's who you are as a person — smart, funny, energetic, compassionate — that's what matters, not what size clothes you wear."

"I can be all that and also like my body. I'm doing this and would appreciate your support. You don't have to follow my plan too." I wrap my arms around her big sweatshirt. We stand to hug for a moment, enjoying the comfort of our friendship. "Coming over tomorrow?"

"Sure I am. You can count on me." Carol follows her BFF to my BMW for a lift home.

CHAPTER 3

Intermittent fasting, Carbs beware!
Exercise. Autophagy's repair.
Turn back the clock, what's the deal?
Miracle molecules promise it's real.

When I Google, I find a plethora of articles: Ads, podcasts, blogs, and scientific papers. Never mind that there's always an expert expounding on a pet nutrition theory. It works for Dot and it makes sense to me. Combining this way of eating with daily workouts should give me back my figure and energy. No one ever died from this, right? Lots of people die from not looking after themselves, though.

At my tidy desk in a corner of the kitchen, my research notes cement into a vision. I'm glad we changed this breakfast nook into an office when we put in the island. I love the view of the backyard. Spring is the best! Fantasies of the fruit trees, daffodils, and tulips in full bloom prepare me to face the day. I straighten with a new dignity and confidence.

"Can you help me prepare for my new diet?" I say to

Carol during the lunch after our morning workout. "I'll need help to clear my cupboards of all carbohydrates — beans, corn, sweet fruit, not only the white stuff we cleared out already, and to shop for high-fat, low-carb foods."

"You know how I am about cleaning cupboards and shopping. I'm made for this job," she says, finishing her sandwich. I love how she's always positive. "But don't get any ideas about me giving up bread."

I am used to Carol's mindset. It would be easier doing it along with someone else, but never mind — I'm doing this. I've changed from an elite athlete into a fat run-down version, without strength or energy, waiting for an inevitable aging disease to take me down. It's pathetic and unnecessary.

On the way home we head over to Whole Foods for my list of Keto-friendly items.

"That's enough to get me going. I'll get some good recipes and finish cleaning out my fridge and pantry. Can we start today?" I ask. "This will be easy because these are foods I love."

While Carol takes the remaining carbohydrates out of my cupboards and fridge, placing them either in the trash or in a box for the food bank, I print off recipes which substitute almond flour for wheat and stevia for sugar. My next shopping trip list is born.

"I can't believe all the food you're tossing, Jeni," Carol says with a vague hint of disapproval, reading the label on a can of tomato sauce. "Can I take these unopened containers, canned goods and the carrots, so I don't have to throw them out? I know the food bank can use them in the Christmas season, but so can I." From the pantry comes the Christmas smell of cinnamon or nutmeg. "Oh, I tipped an open bag of spices, but I picked them up. Sorry," she says.

"Take the whole shebang if you like. I will lose thirty pounds and get my shape back," I say, turning sideways to show my rolls. "I'd like to get out of these baggy hide-the-bulge outfits!" I have to make sure Carol doesn't think I'm body-shaming her into doing this too. That's not my intent.

"Women put on a few pounds as they get older. Just accept it." Carol bags her shirt over her belly with a flash of annoyance.

"They burn fat more slowly because their muscle mass declines. That's why most women take longer to lose the weight than guys, but with long-term weight loss, we're more successful. But I'm not most women. I have plenty of muscle," I laugh, hoping to lighten her mood.

Even though my mind says focus, and my heart screams that I want to reach my weight-loss goal, I am sometimes weak. Like the time I buy a bag of cheese puffs and a Mars bar while refueling. Like the time at the movie theater, a fasting day, when I munch through an entire bag of popcorn. I've lost fifteen pounds; one snack won't hurt. I rationalize — comforting but dangerous. Luckily, as soon as I fall off the wagon, I jump back on. This is too important to my health. Ben would be pleased with my progress.

Carol phones often to check how I'm doing. I drop onto the sofa and sprawl my legs over the far arm and back like I did when we talked as teenagers. Even though she thinks the program is hogwash, Carol encourages because of my loss. She keeps me on track as my mind often drifts to times which drag me down.

"I'm also doing intermittent fasting," I tell her. "On Mondays I'll eat nothing, but drink water whenever I am hungry. Like Dot said, with this high-fat diet, hunger doesn't register the same as when I'm eating sugars. I figure, from Sunday dinner until Tuesday breakfast, I won't eat. You should come over Monday night for a movie to distract me," I babble. "With fasting I'll lose a pound or two a week, you know. It encourages autophagy, the body's way of recycling damaged cell bits, using their proteins to build new cells. Research has shown that this will help protect me from cancer and dementia."

"Okay, okay, I can tell you've been reading articles about this," says Carol, becoming saturated with information. "You had me at Monday movie."

Wow! She hates I'm bursting with enthusiasm. It's hard not to rant when I'm excited that it's working. She's not keen on the process and doesn't care about the science, but notices the results and supports by monitoring our work-outs in a notebook. She packages healthy snacks for those times when she isn't around and knows I will start moping again. It would be hard doing this without support. Even if she isn't taking part or understanding the science behind it, I need her encouragement. I have to report to her and don't want to let her down.

Funny, that is more effective than letting myself down. I realize athletes push themselves in training, not wanting to disappoint the coach or the team. One coach of mine, when I was twenty-five, was extremely demanding. Unsupervised, our women's' team, twice a week, would work three times around the Universal weight machine, skip for five minutes, jump with medicine balls over our heads for thirty repeti-tions, sit against the wall without a chair for five minutes and run thirty flights of stairs with sand-filled inner tubes on our shoulders. If we finished before the senior boys ended their practice, we could join their scrimmage. After that, we practiced for an hour and ended with wind sprints and pushups. We excelled in games and practices because of our coach's expectations. Individual sport athletes may be different, I wouldn't know. For me, it has always been about doing my best for the team.

With cardio, smart eating and intermittent fasting, the pounds fall off in months. I don't smoke or drink alcohol, practices banned with my new diet. My scales are my friend, emphasizing the pounds disappearing. My morning mirror reflects a definite change of shape. Look at that, girlfriend — I'm talking to myself wide-eyed in disbelief. From oval to hourglass! Gone are the middle rolls, replaced with almost-visible abdominal ripples. My waist curves in — I like that better than curving out. I smile and check out my naked body. Breasts are smaller but perkier. Arms are still muscular but have lost diameter. I think I would look okay in sleeveless tops, because there is no loose skin hanging on my upper arm. Flags, I think they call it.

I sense Ben's encouraging presence when I am weak, or tempted to break a fast before completing thirty-six hours. Sensing his pride makes me strong. We are doing this together.

Preparing for my first Christmas without Ben, I'm distracted by the challenge of avoiding carbs and sweets. Christmas was always a favorite family holiday with lots of traditions. We allowed the kids to only open one gift on Christmas Eve, their new pajamas. Family pictures of Christmas morning show them in brand new PJs, year after year. Presents from Darlene had elaborate bows or small objects attached. Gord wrapped his in the first paper he came across. Ben and I spoiled our children with almost everything they could imagine. The rest of the year, we made them work for the requested item, but at Christmas our generosity was legendary. Ben and Gord decorated the outside of our house while Darlene and I did the tree and wrapped the stair rail with evergreens and lights. We watched football games with sodas and chips. Turkey had all the trimmings.

When the children grew up, Ben and I cut back a little on the Christmas extravaganza, but still the tree, turkey and football remained. Some years, Darlene would come with her family and once again we could spoil children, including stockings for them all on the mantle.

My grandchildren are not here for me to spoil this year. Handmade gifts save me a little money while I watch my budget. Carol and I put up a tree.

* * *

During an afternoon workout before Christmas, we spot Dorothy climbing down from the stair master. We catch up with her getting water from the bottle in the lounge.

"Hi Dot, it's been months on Keto and fasting for me, but I'm not seeing results beyond the scales and the return of the waistline," I say holding my tee in to show the change.

"You look slimmer, Jeni; but I told you there is more." Her voice has a unique force of certainty.

"More than diet, fasting and exercise? I knew you were doing something else." I'm excited because this woman doesn't look seventy. When I asked the Life Coach to help me recover the years, she said it was impossible. But Dot has done it. How? This is what I need to learn. I think I could have done the weight loss with many strategies. I'm sure I look younger just from the work-outs and diet, but she has turned the clock back twenty years or more.

"Well, I'll tell you what has worked for me. Mother

Nature is a bitch. She cuts off our estrogen when we finish childbearing and sends us to the junk heap. Our epigenetic layer degrades and old age symptoms creep in. I'll have none of that! I'm getting younger. I read recent discoveries from a Harvard's genetic research team. Dr. David Sinclair, heading that group, is famous for his work with Resveratrol? They are working on regeneration — age reversal," she focuses on me.

"I remember about Resveratrol several years back," I say. "Isn't that found in red wines?"

Carol chimes in, "Now this part is interesting!"

"You would have to drink over forty bottles of red wine to get enough for one day's consumption, so I don't recommend it." Dot's cheeks make pretty crescents of her brown eyes.

"That's how you look as if you're in your forties, when I know you are older than both of us?" I want to know about this and lean closer, but Carol is stepping back. If Dot has had this success, Wow! She has only a few fine wrinkles.

"Yes, in the morning I take the molecules, Resveratrol and NMN, to repair the damage of aging to my cells." It must repair all the cells in her body. That's amazing!

I ask, "What is the rate of age reversal? How much younger do you get?"

"I'm growing eight years younger each year. I began when I first heard of the study three years ago," she says running her fingers through her curly russet hair; a few silver strands glisten in the LED light of the lounge. "If you do the math, I should look about forty-seven now."

And she does. I can't stand still. Where do I sign up?

Carol squirms, "That's not natural. God means us to get older and die. Aren't you afraid of the side-effects?"

"I have experienced no dangerous side effects. I have

more energy than before. I not only look like I'm younger, I can perform as I did at forty-seven. That's more important. Besides Carol, what are the side effects of not rejuvenating? Dementia, arthritis, strokes, cancer, to name a few," says Dot brushing a bushy orange strand behind her ear.

I nod. "It sounds good to me. I'll take supplements to get years back and avoid all those diseases of old age," This might be the fountain-of-youth serum I've been looking for. I trust my gut when I hear about things. If it seems right, I go for it. I'm trusting and optimistic. But I'll check it out.

"Read *Lifespan* by David Sinclair. That's what I did. I got it on audio books and hard copy. It turned my life around," Dot says. "Not all people will want to hear about rejuvenation. Thirty percent of people are content to grow old, even though they know about all the age-related diseases. They don't want to change their vision, but it's simple to stop the aging process. They will think up reasons to justify their thinking. Just warning you. Not everyone will be excited about this. People thought antibiotics, steam engines, and almost all revolutionary discoveries were crazy when they first came out. This is innovative stuff — not for everyone. Make sure you do the research, read the book. These supplements are not cheap; but they are worth it. You would spend money to keep your car in top shape, wouldn't you? Or would you let it deteriorate and end up on the scrap heap? Think about it. You can't afford not to," Dot says with a wave as she leaves the lounge, workout completed.

"She put me off," Carol says, as she pulls on a lock of hair, her voice disapproving. "She sounds like a know-it-all. And did you hear how she dissed me when I was joking about that stuff in wine? You won't get involved, will you?" She laughs to cover annoyance, then bites down hard on her lower lip.

Perhaps there is a twinge of envy with her criticism of Dorothy. There may be history there, of which I'm unaware. Does she think my enthusiasm will drive a wedge between us? She is resentful of the situation. She can have her opinion, but no way is she going to stop me. She offered to be my support system — let's see some support for this.

"Look at her, Carol. There *is* something to it. It's not only because she's strong and fit. She looks amazing. She has her mojo back, and that's what I'm looking for. I understand you are only supporting my choices because you love me. I love you too. If it is too hard for you to do this, when you don't believe it yourself, I'll try to find someone else to support me. We can be friends and work out together, but it's unfair to ask you to help with this. I can't have negativity and still succeed. What are you getting out of this? I want you to be happy too." At this point I reject negative influences. My dormant wits are regrouping and I'm ready for the rest of my life.

"Jeni," she sobs, pulling a strand toward her mouth. "You are the only person who totally accepts me for who I am. You have never pressured me to change. When I am with you, I have a purpose. I am family. If you need me to help with this, I will. I'm trying to understand, but many times I've had my hopes built up about getting back in shape, and so many times they're smashed. I always fail. I'm not strong like you. Not everything comes easy to me. I can't get involved, because it hurts too much to fail. You think I'm happy because I'm always smiling and joking? I'm not. I live alone. My husband left me. I eat to comfort myself. I know it. You think I enjoy being fat? I hate it! I would love to be attractive again. All that crap about not caring is a cover-up. I know you can be beautiful inside and out. Helping you gives me a purpose. Please, let me help."

If I can help Carol by letting her help me, that's a win, win. I wrap my long arms around her and kiss the top of her head. I tuck the straggling wet lock behind her ear and say, "You are my bestie. I'm here for you, whatever you need."

* * *

A flood of articles, pod casts, Ted Talks, and scientific papers appear when I Google "age reversal". Dot and I are not the only ones concerned with this issue. Scientists around the world are discovering ways to age backwards. The baby boomers are the largest market in America. Hundreds of YouTube videos tell mature women how to dress, apply make-up, or have plastic surgery to make themselves appear young again. Who wouldn't want to live fifty years longer if they were healthy to the end? I want to look young again. I want to BE young again with all the strength, energy, and drive that comes with it.

Opposition is at every turn. The cost of the treatments prohibit most women from taking part. The dismissive attitude of Carol and even God. I know Mother Nature wants me to shrivel after fifty, but Carol says God wants people to grow old and die, too. Is shedding thirty pounds enough? My children are in their forties now. They will think this is weird. They expect both parents to pass away. Ben's already gone; I should follow to be with him, they think. The strategies I read about sound promising, but how can one reclaim past years? It is hard to be butting heads with everyone. I could embrace every wrinkle as a sign of some struggle I overcame. I could slow down and smell roses or something. Then it wouldn't matter if I couldn't run up the stairs. I could drag myself up with a rail, or get a home with no stairs. That's what most seventy-year-olds do! Why am I driven to getting back my lost years and finding the joy of being young again? If it's an option — why not?

Scientific research blasts the truth from my computer. I see Dr. David Sinclair, the geneticist from Harvard, whom Dot said 'changed her life'. I order his book, *Lifespan: Why We Age and Why We Don't Have To*. Disease is a symptom of aging, and aging is treatable.

What if I got a year younger in six weeks? I've got my fitness level where I want, and if this program works for me, I'll get the years back too. I don't regret the time when Ben was my focus. Taking care of him was a privilege and special to us both, but those years took such a toll on me. It was not always easy. There were days when I would cry with frustration, get angry, pity myself, dread the future and his inevitable death. But I wanted him with me as long as possible. If I can get the years back without losing my memory of him, why not?

"Carol, you've got to hear this!" I interrupt reading to speed dial my buddy. The morning sun shines through my bedroom window as I sit up in bed. "Sinclair's lab assistant put his mother on this program, and she began her periods again. Now that is age reversal!"

"Sounds far-fetched. How can that be possible? What woman would want that?" she says with light bitterness. Carol is more than skeptical.

"I would, if it means avoiding old age symptoms which, by the way, lead to death!"

CHAPTER 4

> *Maybe seventy, maybe not.*
> *Who cares my age? I'm looking hot!*
> *The alternative to shrivel and die,*
> *So why the hell would I not try?*

I order the supplements Sinclair mentions and they arrive at my door within days. Months pass; people comment on how young I look. A slim person looks younger than a heavy one. They suppose it's because I'm losing weight. If I see the changes on the outside, my internal organs must be healthier too. I have much more energy; I can work for hours. Last week I worked all day, scraping, sanding and oiling a dresser we stored downstairs for decades. I had been putting it off because it seemed an overwhelming task.

I'm getting younger in appearance. But can I perform as I did years ago? That would be the test. Do my activities reflect my new age? What do sixty-year-old women do? What do I want my life to be when I'm forty-five again? How can I fill my life with the passions of my past? These are my reflections as my future unfolds. If I'm gaining back the lost years, and then some, what gives me joy and purpose?

I revisit many hobbies. Knit socks and scarfs don't thrill my teenaged grandchildren, but I hope they will like the trendy pullovers I'm making. My hands used to become numb from a pinched nerve limiting the time I could knit. Now, whenever I watch TV in the evenings, I think of them wearing these to high school.

A cheesecake is too big for one person. I save half to share with Carol and take the rest across the street to my long-time neighbors, Don and Ethyl Kylo. They are elderly and the sweetest couple alive. Our visits hold many cherished memories.

"Thanks dear." She invites me in for tea and takes Don a piece of cheesecake in his study. The two of us talk about our knitting projects in the kitchen and sip our tea. When I tell her what I'm doing with the molecules, she laughs.

Her dear little face wrinkles behind her spectacles, "Be sensible, Jeni. You are a grandmother, just like me. It's time for us to kick back and enjoy the fruits of our labor."

"I don't like to think I've been kicked back. And that's how it seems, Ethyl. They have kicked us to the curb. Not much fruit to enjoy there either, because with the hospital bills, I'll be lucky if I can keep things afloat." I guess she is a person set in her vision to let nature take its course. Sometimes it's best not to explain the regeneration regime. Like Dot said — not everyone is interested!

* * *

As my fitness and confidence return, I join a crowd of seniors who play volleyball at the community center on Mercer Island. They are men, aged fifty to eighty, but a few women too. The calibre of play is excellent; these are my friends. We hiked together. It's been years since I've been out, but seems as I've not been away.

"I'm sorry about your husband passing. He was a fine man," says Gene. They never really knew him, but Ben and I had joined this bunch for several outings.

"I've missed you. How are you doing, Jeni?" says my favorite setter.

"I'm doing okay, thanks Susan. I'm hoping to get back into my old life. Things are the same around here." I toss her a ball to warm-up.

"Nothing much changes. You're looking good. I like your short haircut."

"Thanks. Call me or email if you need a spare for the coed league. I've missed this so much. I don't have a lot going on," I say as we head onto the court to play for the next two hours.

* * *

It's time to test whether I can run with the pack. I look like a younger dog; I bark like a pup, but can I pull the sled with the best of them?

In March, following the next step of my plan, I enter Team Finder for the Huntsman World Senior Games played each year in St. George, Utah. "I'm a middle blocker who can play in the Fifty-Plus or Sixty-Plus divisions. I'm five-foot-ten and have had years of experience at the Huntsman Games," I write. Six-foot was how I always described myself, but gravity and compression have robbed me of two inches. I have reconciled to five-foot-ten. The only team which responds is a competitive Chicago team in the fifty-five plus division. It has been four years since I've played; but I am strong. I'm fifteen years older than these women. I won't know any of the ladies on the Chicago Classics. If I screw up, it won't matter. I won't screw up, but if I did. Just saying. They haven't invited me to stay with them. I need to book a hotel. What am I doing? Really? I qualify for the seventies.

I follow routines of housekeeping like a robot: vacuuming, dishes, laundry, watering plants. My mind flits forward to my athletic challenge. When my home is clean and organized, I am at peace. Ben appreciated the work I did to keep things in order. It wasn't always easy with two busy, messy kids. Carol comes over often to continue coaching and purging, as I make room for the person I am becoming. I focus on my crafts, my diet, and consistent gym workouts. In the mornings, I take my supplements and relish the results.

"You're spending a fortune on those jars," Carol says with disgust as she enjoys a piece of the blueberry cheesecake. "It's a waste of money, if you ask me."

"Not asking you," I laugh. "My money, my molecules, my decision, my consequences."

* * *

"You look younger," says my hairdresser who, for years, has trimmed my graying bleached hair long enough to tie back or put up in a messy bun. "I'm giving you a new modern bob with blond low-lights and ash brown high-lights". The frumpy gray is a thing of the past. I wish I had done this sooner. If I started this whole regime earlier, perhaps it could have saved Ben's life. But cancer grows a long time before we realize symptoms. Even if the molecules are cancer resistant, I doubt if it would cure cancer already established. If it could have, Ben and I would still be together. He would love this new hairdo. I don't know if it will stop the graying and turn back to my original brown, but the current gray will blend in, showing no roots. Stopping by Bartell Drugs, I splurge on eye make-up and a new pink lip stain.

Birds are twittering in the flower-decked trees lining my street, as I bound up the front steps and set parcels on the bench in the entrance. Sun shining into the living room reflects my cheerful optimism as the mirror in the hall holds an attractive smiling woman with a cute hair-do perhaps in her late fifties or early sixties. I busy myself arranging my volleyball excursion. This is where I prove to myself that aging backwards works. If I can keep up with this young Chicago team, I'll know. Then I can plan the life I want to live.

"Carol, I booked my transportation today for the October tournament in St. George, Utah. I used my credit card points so the flight cost twelve dollars in airport fees," I say into my cell phone.

"There are other costs, I'm sure." She doesn't sound excited about my trip.

"There's the shuttle return fare to bus me from Vegas to St. George. I'm booking the Fairfield Inn, right across the street from the principal volleyball venue, the Dixie Center. Therefore, I won't rent a car. They provide a full breakfast and lunch, if I take a bag to sneak leftovers. The tournament fee, a hundred dollars, supplies two free meals. My room will be the greatest expense. Don't you think I deserve a vacation?"

"When will you be going?" she snaps.

"I'm traveling the day before the Games begin and returning the day after the finals: tenth of October to fifteenth. Twelve thousand athletes over fifty compete at the tournament each year in thirty sports; more athletes than at the Olympic Games," I say, hoping she will be excited for me.

I continue, "I'm trying to be frugal. My pensions are barely sufficient. You never know what will come up, now that I'm getting younger and death is not just around the corner."

She laughs. She likes the thought of me being healthy and fit, but refuses to grasp the consequences of regeneration.

While at Rival Fitness, dressed like Carol in spandex shorts with sports bras concealed by drooping sweat-stained tank tops, I sense eyes taking stock of me. I lean over the handlebars of my training bike, fit in contrast to my pal beside me. With bulging muscles and a six-pack he exposes with intention, Eyes wipes his face on the bottom of his sweaty tank top. That's impossible. Women over sixty are invisible. Eyes strides close with the excuse of drinking from the fountain beside my bike. His eyes lock on mine, twinkling blue and compelling, as he returns. His exposed shoulders ooze testosterone.

Carol notices. "You are smokin', Girlfriend. Let's go shopping after we shower."

"I could use a few things. I'm down from fourteen to a ten. My clothes are hanging loose. It would be nice to get some fresh looks for the games, but you know I pack light for sports trips. All I wear there are sneakers and sweats."

"I sense this time will be different, and let's make sure you're ready for anything," says Carol living vicariously. "Now that you look amazing again and are single, start putting yourself back in the action. Take some risks. Flirt. Know what I mean?"

I say, "I don't know if I'm emotionally ready yet. What if

someone is interested? I'm not over Ben and I'm trying to learn to live on my own."

* * *

At home, I strip down and shower after the tough workout. My mind switches to the remarkable thing that happened. That ripped guy was checking me out. How long has it been since that happened? I pull on my peach lace bra and matching panties, lean back on my bed and reach for the big massager, a retirement gift from the pharmacy staff. I run its vibrating domes along my thighs. My muscles still need this after a workout to keep them from stiffening. It's especially good today! I let it continue up the inside of my leg and between my legs. Is age reversal stimulating my libido, or is it that someone thought I was worth smiling at today? Don't care. Damn, that's good! The fabric becomes moist as I guide the machine to the right spot.

Suddenly my orgasm overwhelms me, and I press it harder into my throbbing crotch. Spasms and shivers spread throughout my body. I am more alive than I have been in a long time. I'm overwhelmed with emotion, and the realization that it has been three years since my last orgasm. And since I retired, I've only used this on my back and calves!

When I pick Carol up in my eight-year-old BMW, she listens to my confession and laughs, "You can do better than a Thumper Sport Massager! Let's find you a Real Man."

"If you knew where to look, you'd find one for yourself," I poke. We hurry to the mall.

CHAPTER 5

Can I still do it — be athletic again?
Reach through the challenge, the doubt, and the pain?
Rekindle passion? Oh, yes I can
Catch the eye of a special man.

*I*t's barely above freezing on the tenth of October, when Carol provides an early morning ride via the rainy freeway to the Sea Tac airport. Alaska Air is the first departure terminal. She leaves the engine running in her old red Mazda and hops into the drizzle for a quick hug.

"Let your hair down. Take some risks and have fun," says Carol "You've been uptight for years now. I know the wild, crazy woman is there, and I want to hear all the memorable details."

I'm taking both Ben and her along for this adventure in spirit. My compact backpack carries my sneakers and shorts, which I will need even if my suitcase doesn't make it to St. George. Wet and tousled, I throw her a kiss, hoist my backpack, and steer my wheeled carry-on into the terminal.

With a glance back as she darts into traffic, I leave Seattle behind.

I'm alone in a crowd of bustling travelers. It is a familiar sensation, going off to play with a team. Wearing slim, dark blue, high-waisted jeans, a white jersey tee tucked into a wide white belt with gold buckle, white sneakers, a red denim bomber jacket and gold hoop earrings, I touch the small gold butterfly necklace. It's Ben's last anniversary present. As long as I wear this, he will remain close to me.

With my carry-on checked through, boarding pass and driver's license in hand, I get by security.

"Are you sure you're seventy? Looking good," says the security attendant checking my driver's license. People over seventy-five don't remove their shoes, but that will never be me. Except my birthdate will always be 1950. Already my health span must be near sixty.

I wish Ben and I could have relived our fifties; we had such fun together. We both worked full time, and the weekends brought chores and driving kids to music lessons or sports events. One night a week was date night. Holidays were sometimes as a couple and often as a family. I touch my necklace and imagine him here, walking through the airport. We would laugh, buying magazines and junk food at the bordering shops. Perhaps we'd get a leg massage and complain about the trek to the gate.

I watch a movie on the plane and pull out the nuts, cheese and hard-boiled eggs stashed in my pack. When I land in Vegas, I scurry down slot-machine lined halls to the baggage claim. It's always exciting to see if my bag will turn up, and to examine its condition. Dozens of gray and black carry-on suitcases tour by me on the carousel. When a familiar gray case, sporting a red ribbon, spills out onto the track, I'm surprised I am holding my breath.

We are in Terminal Three. I follow the Web's instructions, taking a shuttle to Terminal One where my ride awaits. This has all gone smoothly. On the same bus to St. George are obvious competitors for the Games: several weathered women softball players, a long gun trap shooter carrying his weapon in an enormous case, a bald swimmer or track athlete and two obvious basketball players. I can tell most sports: the shoes, the caps, and the equipment. It's hard to guess the pickle-ball athletes as they come in all sizes. It's been four years since I've been to the Huntsman World Senior Games. Things could be different.

In daylight, this is a delightful trip. Stretching miles out of Las Vegas, I-15 winds through the barren mountains in a canyon cut by the Virgin River. The sun can't reach us as we scurry after shadows with cliffs on each side. Still in Nevada, it passes through the gambling town of Mesquite, cuts through the northwest corner of Arizona and stretches for St. George. Two hours and a time zone later, we pull into our destination.

The Fairfield has undergone extensive renovations since my last visit. The lobby and the dining area are bright and modern. My room, 320, reveals a king-sized bed, a dresser, a fridge, a desk, but the toilet draws me in. I seldom pass a bathroom without a visit, one symptom of seventy which remains. Throwing on practice gear, my suitcase left open, I hurry across the street to the courts in the Dixie Center. The enormous gymnasium holds a dozen volleyball courts. The excitement of competition builds within my chest as friendly athletes scurry throughout the center. Registration lasts until five o'clock, so I can do that later. My team is on Court Seven. I don't recognize anyone, stifle my anxiety and introduce myself.

"Hi, I'm Jeni from Seattle," I say, pulling up my knee pads

and tossing a ball from the storage basket to another tall player. They are all young with bikini-beach bodies. Adrenaline and anticipation translate into skills dormant for some time. Moving through the drills, I learn their offense and defensive patterns. My serving is reliable, though not as hard as I recall from seasons past.

Volleyball is a simple game. You pass the ball to your setter, who sets for the hitters — duh. These ladies are skilled at passing; the setters hang the ball in the right spot; and it is a dream to sky and pound it down. Sky is jock-speak for jump and for anyone who cares, yes, I can still jump and yes, I can spike the ball. I can dive to get a ball about to hit the floor. I am slower getting to my feet than I remember, but no slower than the rest of my team. They are fifty-five and I belong. They hand me shirt number four, hot pink with white trim and black number.

Their university sports programs considered women's sports comparable to men's. When I attended, there was no sanctioned women's university sport. Called a tom boy or an Amazon, it embarrassed me to win the top high school athletic award, and I would hurry back to my seat and hide the trophy under me. Confidence radiates from each of these women. Only in the last decade have I embraced my love of competitive sports, as no less than a love of music or book club for other women. With the option of reliving my previous decades, I will fill my years with competitive sports. I now stand tall, for 'I am an ATHLETE'. Today I embrace that title. Has it taken me a lifetime for this realization? I tuck my jersey in my bag with a full heart.

"Always check the schedule on-line and be at the court half an hour before game time. Let's be here at seven-thirty for our eight o'clock game in the morning. Great work Classics," the organizing setter says. "Team dinner is at the Rib and Chop next door."

I wipe back tears. I am on the court, playing well again. This part is still relevant; it isn't over. Did I come to St. George to test whether I could still play? Part of me doubted my ability? Obviously, or I wouldn't sense such relief. To grieve the loss of this part of me, after losing my husband, would be unbearable. These are tears of joy. They mix with sweat dripping from my face onto my damp practice top.

* * *

Registration is at the far end of the Dixie Center. Hundreds, perhaps thousands of St. George residents, volunteer each year for a wide range of tasks to ensure the Games run smoothly. Behind long tables, two pleasant women ask to see my identification, and check my name off their clipboard lists.

"Oh, my goodness. Oh, mercy me. What's your secret? You look like you could be fifty," says pleasant lady number one, her gray hair sprayed in place.

"Thanks," I say, not wanting an extensive discussion. I'd love to share my knowledge. I am flattered, but want to yell, "Why aren't you doing the same thing? It could do the same for you!"

"This ID is important. My, it says, this is your tenth year at the Huntsman Games. You already know, you must show your ID at all competitions. It contains a ten-dollar voucher for one of the listed restaurants, and is your ticket to your sport-social," says pleasant lady number two.

"Yes, thank you. And thank you for volunteering. This is a great tournament," I place the lanyard around my neck over my butterfly necklace. We wear the tags at each competition, though I have never seen them checked. Across the hall, I get a red drawstring bag with a plethora of coupons and samples, a t-shirt with the Games logo, maps, and schedules for all the events. I can check out the gift shop later.

The team, still dressed in their practice gear, sit at the Rib and Chop Restaurant next door. I can use my ten-dollar dinner ticket. In the last seat, I order Buffalo wings. Expecting tasty large chicken wings, the sauce hot and slimy — not Keto, surprises me; I eat them anyway. I enjoy being with the ladies on Classics fifty-fives. They are in another phase of their lives. With kids in college, they still have jobs and mortgages. I don't talk about my situation, only listen.

Our leader, Jodi, has printed off the schedule and goes over the details from the captain's meeting. Since this is Mormon country, there are no competitions on Sunday which provide a day off. A geological hike to Snow Canyon is not a break for recuperation. She explains several rule changes. The back-row substitute, the libero, can switch in for any player. She is small and fast with great passing ability. None of this should affect my play. I know I can contribute tomorrow. Our initial match is at eight in the morning.

* * *

My clothes folded and put in drawers, jackets and dresses hung in the closet.

"I will sleep better if I go for a quick hot tub," I say out loud to no one as older folk do, and pull on my cheap purple swimsuit. The pool is open until ten PM, which gives me lots of time to get towels from the desk. The air is warm to me, though the receptionist is complaining about it being too cool.

Several athletes share my idea. The chatter is loud over the noise of the jets. Two older women are neck deep, while three muscular guys in their fifties talk about their opponents for tomorrow's matches. They are all volleyball players.

"When do you play?" The closest of the women goes on, "We're in the sixty-five plus age division and tomorrow we are playing at a high school west of town."

Oh, my God! These are the women *my age*! I could even play seventy-plus. The team I'm with is ten to fifteen years younger, but I'm a better fit with them.

I smile, not wanting to appear judgemental. "I play at eight at the Dixie Center."

"We might get back in time to watch the younger girls play. It's nice to remember when we could move like that. Now we're slower so the games aren't as exciting to watch," the second lady says with amusement. Her face is old but a child still looks out from her eyes.

As they climb out of the pool, I notice the flags under their arms and the expanded waistlines. Their gray hair and lack of make-up confirm the impression they are giving up on their appearance, at least while they are at the games. They seem at ease with themselves. Did aging bring a freedom and acceptance of their bodies, regardless of their condition? Why am I adamant that I must regain the strength and abilities which I've enjoyed all my life? Why can't I accept that it's too much work to struggle against natural aging? What's wrong with aging gracefully? The thought makes me shudder. I'm sorry. I'm not afraid to do whatever it takes to reach my vision.

I'm happy that my life is changing, and it hasn't been

difficult for me. Reversing my age one year in six weeks, with a simple program, makes me wonder why everybody isn't doing it. Perhaps they will when they hear how easy it is.

"We'll see you at breakfast, Rusty," one man says, and two of them head for the gate. Rusty's gaze focuses on me.

He sees me. Not invisible. I smile.

"So you're on a fifty-plus team," I say, opening the conversation.

Rusty says, "Yes, but I'm fifty-six and playing down. I'm playing fifty-five-plus next session."

"I'm Jeni. I'm only playing the first one, fifty-fives. Where are you from?" I ask, changing the subject and moving closer, so I can hear over the roar of the jets. I'd better not move too close or he'll think I'm being forward. Wait! That's one of the old lady tapes. Fifty-year-olds would move right in.

"Portland, Oregon. And you?"

"Seattle, but my team is from Chicago. They needed a middle."

Rusty says, "I play middle blocker too, though our team has so many players, I doubt I'll see much back row action. They'll stick in our pint-sized libero for his passing. Nobody thinks someone six-foot-five can play back row. At home I play all the way around and I love it." His broad muscular shoulders ride above the foaming surface with tiny droplets clinging to the gray chest hair spread between his pecs. Delicious.

"Me too. Luckily, we only have seven players. I may play both front and back. Women never like to sit out. My team is intensely competitive. I hope I can keep up," I say, but remember hearing we have a libero too.

"Oh, you look pretty hot," he says, then looks down in

embarrassment. "I mean, you look strong and fit — like a middle should look. I'm sure you'll play fine."

Blushing, I sense Ben's presence by stroking my butterfly necklace. What would he think about my sexual sensations? "I play the early match tomorrow. I'd better get to bed," I say. The moon, a golden sphere, rises above the buildings and the water jets stop without my noticing.

"Nice chatting with you, Rusty," I say. "Maybe I'll see you play sometime."

"Oh my name is Russ, short for Russell; but my team-mates think Rusty is better for a senior athlete. You might call me Rusty too after seeing me play." His chuckle shows he doesn't think this is true.

"I look forward to it, Russ."

He watches as I step out of the hot tub, my hand touching the rail for balance. Wrapped in my towel, I smile back to see he is following me out.

It's nearly ten o'clock and the pool will close. Perhaps he only stayed there to talk to me. I picture his broad shoulders and narrow hips; his chest with a light dusting of grayish brown hair; slightly receding hairline, tiny dimples and, when he smiles, his blue eyes smile too. I turn around, but he's gone.

I never asked where and when his team plays. What is his team's name? Have I been out of this game so long I don't know how to flirt? I toss my wet towel in the bin by the front desk and head for 320. Now my purple swimsuit is pink. They put too much chlorine in that tub. I'm relieved it's a cheap suit. It was worth it. When I am old, I shall wear purple as the poem goes.

Carol answers immediately as though she was holding the phone knowing I would call.

"I got here okay," I say. "It's in the high seventies during the day. Our team practiced and had dinner together. They're skilled and young. I'm playing in the fifty-fives."

"How is it? You haven't played for four years," she says.

"It's as if I've been playing all along. Stamina is decent, and I'm playing well," I say. "Carol, I met a super-hot guy in the Jacuzzi tonight. We were alone. The others had left. I know his name is Russ, he's fifty-six and lives in Portland," I say, remembering him following me out of the hot tub.

"Tell me more. I like it you're going after the younger guys," she giggles.

"That's all there is. I'll try to give you details tomorrow. Check our team results on-line; we're called Classics. We play in the morning. Take care of yourself, Girlfriend," I say.

"And you be careful, but enjoy yourself and good luck. Good night," she signs off.

CHAPTER 6

Disappointment, success,
Present lost — I must process.
I take risks, but not alone.
Shrunk libido now has grown.

always set out clothes for the next day, which is paramount if sharing a room with teammates. When the alarm sounds at half-past six, I am dressed for competition before I'm awake. Black cotton panties, black sports bra, black spandex shorts, kneepads ready for action, and my hot pink jersey, number four.

From the jar in the fridge I drop a teaspoon of NMN under my tongue where it dissolves. I run a brush through my hair, splash water on my face, and follow with moisture cream. It's so dry here in the desert that my legs are flaky. The chlorine in a hot tub also dries me out. While my face absorbs the cream, I slather it on my arms and legs. I hardly need make-up, only eyeliner and mascara. The age spots don't even need concealer. Another sign that the molecules are working. My age spots are fading. Even the ones on my hands vanished. The pink lip stain is perfect with the uniform. I rummage through my jewelry for my pink gold stud earrings. They will go nicely with the butterfly chain I always wear. My hand goes instinctively to my neck to stroke Ben's gift.

What the fuck? It's not there. With drapes thrown back for maximum light, I pull the bed apart, tossing the pillows and lying on my tummy to look under the skirt. That was useless. The bed is on a platform, so there is nowhere to go. I look anyway before scrambling to the bathroom. Dumping my make-up bag on the counter, I frantically rummage through for a glint of gold. It's not on the floor, with my wet bathing suit, or in the drawers either. Last night I was so distracted by that amazing guy in the hot tub that I didn't even notice that my necklace was missing when I got back. Perhaps it fell in the hot tub, in the lobby, in the elevator or in the hall. My mind races. How can I continue if I don't have the comfort of knowing Ben is with me? There might be a Lost and Found.

"Good Morning," says a cheery voice at the front desk when I phone.

"I've lost a gold butterfly chain. Is it at the desk or Lost and Found? It's awfully important to me," I say.

"Wait a moment and I'll look." Lengthy pause. "Nothing here at the front desk, I'll check the Lost and Found when it opens and if it's there, I'll leave a message for Rm. 320. Okay?" Cheery Voice says.

"Okay," I agree.

* * *

My team meets on court five in an hour. I can't let them down. Quickly, I pull on sport socks, marked with an L and

R to show the foot. I tie my sneakers with a double knot, so they won't come loose during the game. I should wear sandals and carry my shoes, but I'm so focused once I get to my gear that I don't care if I track in sand later.

Maybe Russ will be at breakfast because his friends said they would see him there. The kitchen has been serving for an hour and the aroma wafts down the corridor. My plate has two sausage patties, scrambled eggs and strawberries. The friendly buzz of excited players does nothing to cheer me while the dining room bustles with seniors in many team uniforms. My heart would leap if he were here; but with his absence, my spirits sink lower. I wolf down my food alone and make a second round to stuff a zip-lock bag for lunch.

Fox News is interviewing someone; a TV hung above the neighboring table. Thankfully, the sound turned off, eliminates that distraction. It's bad enough that Russ isn't here and that I've lost my necklace. I need to stay focused.

At court five, our captain Jodi passes with our second setter, Kate, and the rest are in various stages of preparing for warm-up. Two hitters are tying their shoes. Tammy, pulling off sweatpants, wears a black libero shirt as she talks to a woman whom I recognize from the sixty-five division. Oh, our team has a libero. This means I'll substitute out in the back row. My mind races to my conversation with Russ last night. A warm glow flows through me as I think of his confidence and dynamic vitality. I like to play back row too; I remember saying. Chances are, I won't see any back row action. I don't wear sweats but toss my unzipped navy hoodie on a chair over my backpack. St. George is chilly in the morning and sometimes the gym is drafty too. The older woman, who was talking with Tammy, stops with a curious smile. "How do you keep up with these women?" she puzzles.

I blurt out, "I'm taking something that makes me younger. It seems to work." I would like to explain molecules, but it is warm-up time.

She tosses "good luck" in my direction. Was she being sarcastic? Does she think I'm out of my league?

"You ready to pass?" asks Julie, my warm-up partner from practice yesterday drawing my attention away. She is the second middle, my opposite.

"Let the games begin," I say, grateful to be part of this group.

After ten minutes of passing, hitting, and serving our teams line up on the end line of the court. When the referee signals, we run down the sideline and along the centerline, offering our opponents firm handshakes under the net. Excitement mounts as I'm surrounded by athletic women who have travelled thousands of miles for these games. We gift bookmarks with all the teams' names for our division, thanks to Tammy, who apparently enjoys making these attractive items. The opponents give us Halloween suckers, which we throw in our bags.

Diggin' Life from New Mexico, one of the weaker teams, offers an excellent opposition for my first match. I'm uncertain at first. It has been four years since I've competed, but ten years since I've played for a team this strong. When I receive the first serve, it blasts off my rigid arms into the abyss.

"No worries," Jodi gives an encouraging smile. "Get the next one."

I let a deep breath spread through me and imagine I'm playing at Mercer Island. Those guys serve hard and play a fast game. It's about skill, not age or gender. I get more than my share of sets. I focus on position, always being ready for the next block or hit.

While I relax and enjoy the tempo, we concentrate on our offense. Returned balls are often erratic. The speed and passing of our team is impressive. The setting is high, the way I like it. Even the shorter players are hitting hard. The enjoyment of playing at this level again astonishes me. Adrenaline courses while a beaming smile imprints on my face. We win both games.

We have the nine o'clock match on the same court, which goes even more smoothly as I gain confidence. Our team is in sync and positive. When it ends, we divide up work duties for the next hour where we provide the score-keepers, libero-tracker, down-ref, and linesmen at the same court. I grab a flag and line the first game; then in the second game, Tammy takes my flag, leaving me free for half an hour.

From the bleachers on court one, I watch the first Global Cup match between Germany and Italy. Men over fifty, representing six countries, play a small tournament and entertain a sizable crowd. They alternate years with the over-fifty international women's teams.

A fine time to eat; I pull out my zip-lock bag. Germany leads Italy fourteen to eight, and the enthusiastic fans for both teams chant in their native tongues. It's hard to believe these men are over fifty. They are jumping and hitting as hard as university players. I'm mesmerized by the speed of play. Germany wins twenty-five to fifteen, and the cocky victors quickly dismiss the congratulatory center line meeting with the Italians. Time's up for me too. I toss my trash in the nearby bin and glance back to my team.

Over on court five, the match finished, Jodi is flipping a coin with the ref for the choice of side or service. We win service and move our gear to the other bench for warm-ups. Tammy looks at me quizzically as we pass under the net. What did that older player tell her? Obviously that I'm seventy, and I will be the weak link on this competitive younger team when we have our next match. How can I prove I've reversed my age if I don't fit in on a younger team?

Our opponent, Roof, ranked number one, will probably be a finalist. I'm starting in position three, center front as before. The hitters opposing us are five-foot-ten, six-foot and six-foot-one. Their six-two offense often leaves deep back corners unprotected. Also, a short area behind the blocks, vulnerable to drop shots, requires a quick mobile defense. I'm still smiling as I analyze their weaknesses.

It's a close affair with the teams trading lead throughout. Nothing hits the floor; our rallies are long. Each point is a struggle. With a deep breath, I tip my head forward, squint across at my opponent, and dig deep into untapped resources of strength. Who was it that said, "Winning isn't everything; it's the only thing?" We split with Roof: twenty-five to twenty-three, twenty-three to twenty-five. That's as close as it gets! I hope Tammy has decided that I'm good enough. I am playing my best so there isn't anything else I can do, anyway.

Jodi, our coach and captain, says in the huddle after the match, "That's where we want them. We will get continually stronger. Now we know how they play; we'll be ready for them in the finals."

Heading right into our next match, I'm glad I ate earlier. I refill my water bottle from the orange barrels on tables at the side of the gym. White towels on the floor catch the overflow as athletes fill in a hurry. They schedule the twelve courts to begin on the hour. Between games becomes a busy time with seniors rushing for water and bathroom breaks.

The constant screech of referee whistles blends as white noise. Conscious of the smell of sweat and old running shoes, I hurry past the seventy-plus men's' game. These guys are my age, yet seem much older. The bald heads, white beards, and rippled skin set them apart from the younger guys. Only a few of their teams play better than the best seventy women's teams. Almost everyone on their court has a brace — knees, elbows, taped shoulders.

Our team sprawls on the chairs at our court, using this time between games to recover. We let our opponents take the ten-minute warm-up without us. We need cool-down, not warm-up. Luckily, a weaker team practices serving. I set down my water bottle and shag some of their balls. I prefer not to rest — someone has to chase down practice balls which skid under the net barrier between courts.

They call our opposition "Never Give Up". Who would name their team that? It doesn't infuse fear in the opponent. The result is as expected. Classics end the day with a seven win, one loss record. I'm exhausted now; not hurting, but tank-dry and pleasantly bagged. Tammy watches as I wipe my face with a towel. She probably wonders if I will collapse with a heart attack or something.

Actually, one year at this tournament, a fellow who had been dancing at the social the night before, died of a heart attack on the court next to our game. They summoned a competing doctor who couldn't revive the healthy looking sixty-two-year-old. What a way to go — doing what you love to do — suddenly, among friends!

* * *

I stop at the bleachers at Court One. USA plays Mexico. Mexico is fast but their players are physically not a match for the tall powerful US men. Volleyball has not been a men's sport in all US universities since Title Nine, when women's programs became funded equally with the men. Allen Allen, with a thirty-six-inch vertical, from the University of Hawaii Rainbows became captain of the US Olympic team. Their arch rivals, UCLA, was coached by Al Scates, for decades. Now, I recognize none of these players. The sheer population of the US allows a pool of thousands of athletes from which to form their team, while countries like Mexico can only name a hundred available candidates.

But it doesn't mean I can't enjoy watching them all. My eyes rivet on the calf of a hitter. When he smashes the ball, his leg is bent at the height of the bottom of the net. I am drooling over the pecs drenched under a white singlet; the six-pack that exposes as the blocker stretches his arms to defend. Not people to know; but here for my sensual enjoyment. When did watching athletic prowess become sexual?

"That was amazing," a voice beside me states, breaking me free of my fantasy.

"Yes, great hit." Still wearing my cemented smile, I turn to the voice. Obviously, a softball player, still in stained white pants from sliding around the rust-colored diamonds of St. George. He stopped in at the gift shop to buy the new hat he holds which reads Huntsman on the brim. He heard the volleyball match in the nearby gym. I need not ask, since I already know — but I do.

"What's your sport?" I say, practicing my flirt, which wasn't up to scratch last night. "How was your game today? What position do you play?" I'm on a roll. Now that he's talking, I hope there isn't a quiz, because I'm thinking about my next question. Focus Jeni. Something about, "Did you already get lunch?"

"Yes, I ate at eleven," I say as my stomach growls, and we both laugh.

"If they had showers here, I'd take you out for dinner." He's staying with his team at some condos, but he has a car.

"Why, I'm right across the street," I say. "I want to shower before dinner too. I could invite you for a shower, if you brought a change of clothes — only for a shower." This is one of those risky moves Carol recommended. Often people, on the last day when someone has already checked out, will shower in another athlete's room. This does not seem like a strange offer to me.

We pick our way carefully down the bleachers and walk, bags in hand, across the street, awkwardly into the lobby of the Fairfield.

"Wait!" A plate of chocolate chip cookies sits on the reception counter. Normally I'd pass — but one won't hurt. They smell irresistible. It's been a long time since I've eaten chocolate chips — heavenly! I nod and Tom, that's his name, takes one to eat on the way to my room.

I'm glad the maid has cleaned, remembering the search for my necklace and the mess I left. My heart sinks as I consider what Ben would say, if he knew I had a man showering in my room. But Ben isn't here. There is no message light flashing to show that my cherished butterfly necklace is in the Lost and Found. I hold my hand against my throat.

"You go first. I must decide what to wear," I say, opening my drawer and choosing my white lace bra and panties. Tom stuffs in the cookie's last bite, and soon I hear the muted sound of the shower.

It might be nice to step in and enjoy a back wash. Carol would encourage it, I know, but I'm not feeling it. The white cotton jersey dress will go well with my sandals and butterfly — no, not the necklace. Like a tongue abrading constantly on a chipped tooth, my hand moves to my neck, reminding of the loss of my husband, searing pain through my heart. I'll wear my hoop earrings and need nothing more. I turn on the TV as Tom comes out, fresh and young in blue jeans, wearing his free Huntsman Games t-shirt.

I hand him the remote, take my stack of clothes and say, "I'll only need ten minutes."

When I step back into the room, Tom rises from my bed, whistles and, as promised, leads me out to dinner. Across from the Dixie Center is his parked rental car. Everything is within blocks — a major reason for choosing the Fairfield. It's fun to be strolling along in the warm evening, making small mindless chatter with a friendly stranger.

"I thought I knew the best restaurants in St. George, but Magelbys is a recent addition," I say as we drive across Highway Fifteen and into their parking lot.

"While you were showering, I made reservations," he says.

"I'm glad, because this place is hopping," I say loving it from the moment we enter: white cloth tablecloths, bustling waiters, racks of desserts in glass displays. "It smells like my kind of food. There's something about Italian spices that beckons you to order the minute you step out of the car."

I order steak, medium rare, artichoke and spinach dip with vegetables instead of bread, roasted broccoli with double butter and sour cream.

"Sounds good. I'll have the same," Tom says, handing the menus to the waiter who gestures to another, carrying a pitcher of water.

"How long have you played softball," I ask.

"Since I was ten, I guess. I played fast pitch until the last ten years. It's slow pitch at the Huntsman Games. I'm an outfielder. There are four on the field in slow pitch, and we see a lot more outfield action than in fast pitch. That slow arched pitch is easy to hit," he says.

"I learned volleyball in high school but never played competitively until I turned fifty. There is a skilled group in Seattle who play twice a week, and several night leagues," I say. "Tomorrow night is our sport's dinner-dance. What does softball do for a social?"

"It's more like a beer garden. It's open only to the softball players and wives, if they get tickets. Pulled pork on a bun served with a salad. Players don't go for the food and they don't serve beer," he laughs, stuffing his last bite into his mouth. "Want to share dessert?" Tom points at the waiter and says with his mouth full.

I see huge portions of cake going to other tables. "Only if it's crème Brule," I say, but that's not on the menu. I've been having a dickens of a time eating wisely on this trip, and can never resist crème Brule.

"I'm sorry I used my dinner ticket yesterday, Tom," I say, tipping my head to one side when the bill comes.

"Don't even think it. It's my treat. I don't get to take a beautiful woman out that often," he says.

Why would that be? He's nice, fit, tall and not bad looking. He talks with his mouth full, but what else am I missing? We listen to golden oldies on the radio on our way back to the hotel. Perhaps he knows my age and has a fetish for seniors.

Instead of dropping me at the door, he parks the car. It's early and I hate being alone. I invite him in to watch a movie. When he closes the drapes, it is light outside, but now dark in my room. No messages blink on the phone. I turn on the bedside lamp and grab the remote.

"Let's see what movies are on." I settle on the recent

Spiderman movie. Propping up the pillows, Tom snuggles at my side.

"Mind if I loosen my jeans?" he asks. "I ate too much."

"Make yourself comfortable," I say with hesitation and see in my periphery that he is undoing his belt and jeans snaps, pulling his t-shirt loose over top his opened pants.

I'm getting into the plot, a young Spiderman trying to learn to control his powers and earn his outfit. His antics are hilarious and I'm engrossed in the movie. Tom moves my hand to his lips and kisses tenderly. How sweet. Warm breath on my neck draws my attention away and the old familiar urges surface. He licks my finger tips and one by one sucks on them. My goodness! It feels erotic. I shouldn't be wanting this.

He turns off the bedside light and settles beside me, panting. I can barely see, but Tom's eyes are closed, and a sappy look masks his face.

"We're missing a hilarious movie. I can't do this, Tom," I say pulling myself back to reality. He just moans.

Carol would approve that I'm getting some proper action, but it doesn't feel right to give in to lust. This guy isn't a suitable match for me. Not like Ben was. He could never take Ben's place.

"Your thighs are so firm," he growls as he rubs and pinches my leg. "I love flat abs." He breathes heavily as he rubs my tummy through the fabric of my dress. I remove his hand.

Curious what turns a guy on, or how they try to turn on a woman. His hand moves to stroke my breast. I notice that my nipple is erect, as is he, growing ever more so, and pushing against my side. As I push him away, he climaxes, wetting not only his jeans but the side of my dress.

"Damn, I'm so sorry," he says and embarrassed rushes to the bathroom to clean, tucking himself back in his pants.

"No biggie, Tom," I say. It's gross. Premature ejaculation is not in novels, where men are dominant lovers and women scream for more. The women jump up on tables, while they rip off each other's clothes. Chemistry, I suppose.

When he comes out, flushed miserably, I say in a clipped voice that forbids questioning, "You should leave since you didn't hear I wasn't interested. You aren't into this movie and I play a nine o'clock game." It's only seven-thirty when I close the door behind my humiliated guest.

I throw my dress in the laundry bag, slip into my comfy PJs, rinse out my uniform in the sink, and finish the movie before I call Carol with the details of my day.

"Hi Jock," she answers. "How'd your day go? Going to the gym sucks without you."

"Carol, I've lost the butterfly chain Ben gave me for our anniversary. I've searched all over. It's breaking my heart," I sob.

"I know the one. That's too bad. I hope it will turn up. Now tell me the up-lifting parts of the day," she says, trying to cheer me up.

"Well, our team did well. We split with a powerful team called Roof. They'll make it to the finals, and we might too. One of our players has found out how old I am, and she's watching my every move — waiting for me to screw up. But guess what strange thing happened," I continue, not waiting for her answer. "When I was watching the Men's Global Cup, a handsome softball player hit on me. After showering in my room, he took me out to dinner."

"What? You invited a stranger back to your room to take a shower? Are you crazy?" she laughed.

"You haven't heard the best part yet. After dinner, I

invited him in to watch a movie. I was watching Spiderman, and he was playing Spiderman beside me. Being seduced is confusing now that my sexy is waking up. He ignored my attempts to settle him down. I didn't want to make out, but I can't believe his efforts to get me excited, pinching my leg and rubbing my stomach like he was taking inventory or something. He got so excited, when he reached for my bra he came all over himself, and the side of my dress. I'll never wear that dress again without thinking about him," I say giggling.

"If you didn't like him, why didn't you stop him?" She's trying to stifle a laugh.

"I don't know? Flattered at the attention. Curious, and he seemed harmless, I guess. He got my interest, and I encouraged him. But when I thought of Ben and what real love-making is like, I pushed him away. I sent him packing." I'm happy there is someone to share this gross adventure.

"I thought you'd hunker down with what's-his-name." she says.

"I didn't even see Russ. So many athletes and playing venues are at this immense event. Even though he's staying in the same hotel, I may never see him again." The perfect clarity of this sends a dreadful chill through me. "I thought you would be proud of me, reaching out for some action, anyway."

"I said enjoy yourself and take risks, but be careful. I guess you came out of that one unscathed, but slimed," she manages a choking laugh, and I can't help but laugh with her.

"I'll call tomorrow again, same time. Who knows what the new day will bring?"

CHAPTER 7

Life will beat me down some more —
Alone, self-doubt, disgust in store.
Just a glimpse of him, court two,
Is not enough to see me through.

 ay two of the tournament, they schedule our matches in a gym near Hurricane, a city twenty miles east of St. George. There are hundreds of volleyball teams this year. They use four venues with the finals all back at the Dixie Center. The teams take their turns playing in alternate gyms. The fine people of St. George provide a shuttle to pick me up at the hotel after breakfast.

We officiate the nine o'clock match, play at ten and eleven in the morning, work at noon and play at one. One gymnasium, with two courts, features our fifty-five plus games. Leaving my backpack against the wall with my team's equipment, I explore the one next door while I wait for our turn to play.

The atmosphere in the other gym is notably different. Instead of balls being passed, players hitting the ball repeatedly against the wall, and athlete's bustling energetically to prepare for warm-ups; on the next-door courts, players stand chatting with balls in their hands. Until warm-up begins, many rest in chairs sorting their gear. Interactions are common between players who have been opponents for many years. These are the seventy-year-old women. Comparing to my younger division — what a difference! Even the warm-ups are slower with less chatter. A few old friends come up for hugs, letting me settle on a chair at the sidelines while competition begins.

How are these women different from the Classics in appearance — from how I look? I've known these ladies for decades, and haven't noticed the gradual changes, but my absence and transformation make the contrast remarkable. It isn't only the fitness level. Some of these friends play almost daily, indoors or at the beach. Their lifestyles stress their bodies with good biological effects, a process known as hormesis. Others show signs of arthritis and inflammation. I know half a dozen widows who have replaced loneliness with this activity. Some remarried. There is no shortage of positive attitudes in this gymnasium. Everyone is enjoying their passion for volleyball and is a cheerful bunch. But, I'm sure every one of them would trade their body for the one they had ten or twenty years ago.

A few still color their hair and others have attractive white styles. In most cases, it is short or pulled back and paid no mind. Noting their mobility, the older players react slower. Players stand more erect and flat-footed, requiring a second motion of bending the knees before moving to the ball. Though experience has increased their ability to expect where the ball is being directed, execution of the pass or set results in broken plays. Few women are hitting hard, serving overhand, or blocking. The game has become one of strategy and placement.

On the best teams of this age, few women carry extra pounds. Those invited to a top group are skilled and fit. Most of the older players on weaker teams show evidence of diets containing sugar and alcohol, or sun damage — arthritis, inflammation, cellulite, and wrinkles.

I am avoiding the aging process but sorry my friends do not have the advantage of these benefits. If I'm playing in a lower age division, how can I share it with them? I remember the excitement of seeing how Dot turned back the clock. Will these people want it explained? Or will they brush it aside and think I'm crazy? If people see age reversal working effectively in the lab, if they see people like Dot and me succeeding, would they not at least be curious?

I leave for the other gym, to adjust to the speed of play of the younger women. It is too easy to settle for a slow game, reserving as much energy as possible for — for what? Now, I am energized. I want to give my best on every play.

I move well in the morning matches, which are easy wins. During warm-up for the afternoon games, Jodi says, "Jeni, you will sit out this match. We will not use a libero."

"Okay, no problem," I'm sitting on the bench alone while Tammy sets and Jodi plays my position at middle.

What the fuck! She will show me how it's done? I'm not needed here! She knows I don't fit in. Tammy probably told her to give her head a shake — a seventy-year-old playing on this team! I'm fifteen years older than they are. I watched my age group play this morning. Who am I kidding that I can keep up? My thoughts rage miserably. In the finals, I'll probably sit out the entire match. This is a warning, so it won't upset me. But I am upset! This game is close. I'm glad I'm sitting out because I'm not as strong as these youthful women. I was probably holding them back when I was on the court. My blood pounds, causing my face to grow hot with humiliation.

A tap on my shoulder gets my attention. Alice Mallot, the tournament director, beckons me to follow her. No problem. I'm not needed here, anyway.

"Jeni, something was brought to my attention and I need to ask you about it," Alice says, when we are on a free court and out of earshot. Alice is a short, energetic blonde who has been running these tournaments for at least eight years. I listen curiously as she continues. "Have you been using drugs to enhance your performance?"

"What? That's ridiculous. I don't drink or smoke and I don't use drugs, Alice. I don't even use any prescription drugs. I take NMN and Resveratrol, various vitamins and melatonin. That makes me healthy and energetic, which might give me an athletic advantage over some, but nothing illegal."

"We need you to report to the medical room after this match for a test — standard procedure for any reported drug use." She turns and leaves me with my heart pounding. If I test positive, it will disqualify my team for every game in which I play. I know I have done nothing wrong. Should I tell the captain? I'll bet they never even noticed I wasn't on the bench.

As they come off the court, I force a smile, ashamed of my thoughts. After shaking hands with our opponent, we gather at our bench.

"Great playing Tammy," says Jodi. "There is still one game of pool play, but not until Monday morning."

"Let's shower, meet at court one and go through the health screening together," says Kate. Some are enthusiastic; others decline.

University students in physical education and health programs administer a series of fitness and wellness evaluations, gathering data on seniors. It gives athletes a baseline for comparison as many of us return annually. This year the screening tests will give me some idea of the success of my nutrition and regeneration programs.

"The social is tonight at seven," I remind them.

At two, the shuttle picks us up in front of the Hurricane venue and returns us to our hotel, where I dress in a t-shirt and shorts for the health screening across the street.

Dixie Drive borders with flowering trees, but their fragrance doesn't mask the sewage and run-off which flows beneath the road-side grates. It reminds me of a favorite vacation spot with Ben. Thailand has blazing sun and odor. St. George has the same, plus brick-red soil surrounding the buildings and extending to the hilltops.

At the front desk in the Dixie Center I ask, "May I book a shuttle to pick me up for the social?" A motherly volunteer hands me a clipboard. I smile at three old gentlemen, the drivers, who patiently wait for assignments on a row of chairs. Carpeted halls of the Dixie Center are lined with vendor's booths selling products which appeal to mature athletes: liniment, orthotics, braces, tape, etc. One sizeable room has registration, one the gift shop, and one a trainer's room. For three days, they set aside many other spaces for Health Screening, free to all the athletes.

The trainer's room is also the medical station which deals with injured athletes and, apparently, drug testing.

"Alice Malot, director of volleyball, asked me to come for a drug test," I say as calmly as possible. All eyes turn to process this statement. Here is a probable cheater. We've never seen what a cheater looks like. So, she looks like that? A young woman hands me a container and follows me to the washroom where, at least, I have the privacy of peeing in private. I wash my hands, hand her the sample and return to the task in the next room.

Each year I do screening, and each year I am told I am obese. But not this year; I weigh one hundred and sixty-three pounds. I'm still strong with the grip of a fifty-year-old man; my hearing is acceptable; blood pressure, one twenty-eight over seventy-three; my cognitive wellness, twenty-one out of twenty-two; BMI, twenty-four point seven: but the best news of all is, for the first time in over a decade, I'm not obese. I'm in the healthy weight range — not even over-weight! Thank you, Keto. Thank you, Dr. Sinclair. So many health problems are common to overweight people. If I live a long life, I want it to be healthy.

My teammates get flu-shots, which I've already had, so I wander into the volleyball area. No more Global Cup competitions today. Oh, my God! A soft gasp escapes me. Russ is playing on court two. Amazed at the thrill as my heart races, I settle unnoticed on the sidelines. He takes charge of the play with quiet assurance. The execution of every move shows competitive focus and skill. His team is winning the first match. Drops of perspiration cling to his damp forehead. Gracefully he dances to block on one corner and backs to cover center, takes a short approach to hit a "one" out of the hands of his setter. Jodi and Kate join me.

"The middle blocker?" says Jodi.

"Is it that obvious?" I say blushing.

I want to stay, but my teammates tell me I must get ready for the social. His face becomes animated when he notices me rise to leave, which causes my heart to sing with delight. I know he wants me to stay. Torn by conflicting emotions, I follow my friends and watch the disappointment register on his strong rigid profile. If he comes to the social, I can be with him there.

* * *

The volleyball dinner/dance fills an old barn which has smooth concrete floors and whitewashed walls and ceiling. We show ID at the door and receive tickets for a random draw. The line forms for the food. I drop my red denim jacket on a chair with my teammates and grab a plate. Oh great, this year it's pasta with meat sauce, Cole slaw and a bun. I skip the pasta and bun and double up on coleslaw and meat sauce. A western band playing Achy Breaky Heart doesn't sound like Garth Brooks, but in a cleared area in front of the band, a line-dance gathers. The rest of the room has fingers of long tables covered with white paper. Hundreds of folding chairs are home to the butts of a myriad of gray-haired or balding partiers, their bottles of water balancing along the table tops. Because there is no liquor served, some players avoid these socials. They can't imagine not having a beer with their dinner after a game day.

My red cotton jersey dress is naked without my necklace. However, I'm the only one who notices. Several of the bald gentlemen ask me to dance. I dance with a scrawny elderly gent who jives as smoothly as wheat in a summer breeze.

"I remember dancing with you four or five years ago and have missed you. Why weren't you here? This is my only time to dance. My wife's in a wheel chair." He must be eighty at least.

"My husband was ill and passed away last year." He swings me into a closed position. I'm comforted as I move to the music held, even by strangers.

"Sorry for your loss. I'm glad you returned." He walks me back to my team's table when the song ends.

"You look like someone who could be a friend of mine," interrupts a cheery voice as I'm gossiping at our table with Kate. Tammy is further down our group, probably telling everyone my age. I turn to see the handsome rugged face of a Steve Martin doppelganger.

"Perhaps you're right," I say as I let him lead me onto the dance floor. It's a foxtrot which he executes adequately. The rest of the evening I spend with Al who turns out to be decent at east coast swing, waltz and polka. We move out of the way when the line dance folk make a mass eruption or the conga line weaves through the crowd.

A member of the American Global Cup coaching staff, he offers a ride home. I cancel my shuttle and move to his table. Eyebrows raise as we leave together. Kate gives me a thumbs up.

It is strange. In my life at home I would not consider taking a ride from a stranger, let alone inviting him into my room. But in the atmosphere of trusting and caring at the Huntsman Games, strangers unite in friendship and cama-raderie because of their love for the same sport. They share the freedom of being away from responsibilities. They are lonely, missing their loved ones, enjoying their passion and being young again, if only for a week. It's a fantasy world and they are all fantasy players, embracing people they wouldn't cross the street to greet at home. When Al gets me back to the hotel, I invite him in.

I wonder why Russ didn't come to the social. Last night's Don Juan was pathetic. Now, I'm here with this fellow who runs out of witty conversation and starts pawing at me. I put some music video channel on the TV and decide I might as well enjoy this. When did a man last treat me as a woman?

Ben was such an attentive lover; always satisfied me before letting himself go there. Or if he came first, he would hold and caress me until I reached orgasm too. We had an amazing sex life until he got sick. My hand searches for the reminder missing at my throat.

"That's when I wanted to be an engineer," Al says. There are other details about him, but I'm somewhere else, with Ben.

"You know you're beautiful." Now he has my attention. He strokes my neck and moves in closer beside me. "I'd love to make you feel loved. Would you like that?"

His hand moving up my thigh shows he isn't waiting for permission. Do I want to get into this mess again? I will eventually. There might not be opportunities for romance when I return to Seattle. My life there is routine and boring. Hormones are raging right now. What the hell. His lips are on my neck and his hand is moving closer to my moist crotch. It seems all right.

The music is smooth and rhythmic; Al extinguishes the light beside the bed. Definitely the right atmosphere. As I'm getting into this, Al undoes his belt, his zipper, and pops out this monster of a penis. He stretches my panties aside and rolls over on top of me. My legs automatically wrap around his hips and there he is, thrusting and moaning. I'm in shock. I never turned Ben away. I should have thrown this guy off the bed when he made his first move. I'm swimming through a haze of emotions and desires. Thankfully, it doesn't last long as he drops beside me on the bed.

"That was beautiful," he says. "I never get that excited at home."

"You're married?" His words register on my dizzied senses. I can't believe a married man would want to have sex with me. Ben and I were always faithful. We needed no one else. I would never resist his sexual advances, which were always considerate and gentle. For years I've had a low libido and been invisible to men. I was so involved in my loss and keeping my life private that I never asked about Al's home life. Stupid and submissive.

"Yes. Aren't you?" he asks.

"I think you should leave. You got what you came for," I say, shaking my head as it cradles in my trembling hands.

Straightening his jeans, he runs his fingers through his hair and says, "I heard that you were the woman who was taking enhancement drugs. If you were cheating at that, I figured you'd be up for a little action." He leans towards me and winks. "I was right. Do you want to meet tomorrow after Global Cup?"

I shut the door behind him. Unbelievable! He has the nerve to ask me out after that? He couldn't even see how upset I am.

Tears rush down my cheeks. I throw myself on the bed. Low racking sobs muffle in the pillow. I feel sick, used, lost, and disgusted with myself. I've lost Ben's necklace. Today my team said I wasn't strong enough and sat me on the bench. They're all going to see me as an old woman now that Tammy has told my team I'm seventy. I may get the team disqualified if I test positive for drug enhancement. It will ruin my reputation here. They may ban me from future games. Tonight, I let some married man have his way with me — like trash, used and discarded. Am I so desperate for affection I invited this kind of treatment? I didn't even enjoy it. And he didn't buy me dinner! This thought makes me smile despite my pain; I call Carol to share it with her.

"Hi Girlfriend. How'd today go? Did you find the necklace, see Russ?" Silence. "Jeni, what's wrong?" She knows when I'm quiet that I'm upset.

"I had the worst day. No, I didn't find the necklace. I saw Russ playing, but I had to race off with my team to the social and he didn't come to the party. I never even talked to him. Also, this morning I was playing great, I thought, until the captain told me I was sitting out the afternoon game. It was a tough match. I don't know what that means."

"It means someone else played your position. You are the new girl on the block, lucky to have a position," she says.

"You're right; but I feel like crap. And I had a drug test. They think because I'm playing this well for someone my age, I must do some illegal drug."

Carol laughs. "You doing drugs? That's crazy. You're not even using aspirin, right?"

"Not. But sometimes supplements make the readings positive, depending on what substances it includes. What if I get my team disqualified? They could ban me from the games entirely." A flash of nausea churns my stomach. "You know what else happened?"

She laughs, "You will tell me; so go ahead."

"The guy I was dancing with offered me a ride home from the Social. I invited him in. I know. Stupid move after last night. He seduced me and after told me he's married. He's on the US Global Cup coaching staff. He had heard about the drug incident, which is why he wanted to meet me. The bastard, and he didn't even buy me dinner." I laugh hysterically until tears pour down my cheeks. My misery is a physical pain which humor won't mask. My throat tightens with a suffocating grip.

"You need me there, not to be your wingman, but to make sure you don't do too many of these stupid things," she says when she hears my laughter turn to sobs.

"I'm a total mess. I should come home and forget this

crazy dream," I'm overwhelmed by the torment of the past few days.

"You're staying and turning this thing around. You'll be better in the morning, I promise," she says.

I pause and breathe deeply. Carol's words instill a calming effect. I swallow hard and manage a feeble answer. "Thanks, buddy. Good night." I rinse out my uniform, set the alarm, and clouded with uneasiness, turn out the light.

CHAPTER 8

Sunday's field trip, with a group,
Lets tired bodies' strength recoup.
Risking company and fun,
Searching for that special one.

he men are wearing black suits and the woman, a cotton dress with puffed sleeves in a pastel blue. They appear out of place, entering the breakfast area where the Huntsman Games athletes replaced their uniforms with tank tops and hiking shorts for their day-off retreats to the mountains. Perhaps there is a wedding or funeral to attend. Holy petunia, it hits me! They are going to Church. It's Sunday morning and these are probably Utah travelers staying at the hotel; not part of the Games.

I survey the room for Russ to no avail. The suited Mormon is in front of me as I skewer a piece of ham and pile eggs on my plate. A wave of guilt washes over me. Is God upset with my behavior last night? I'm wearing tan shorts and a sleeveless shirt, immodest compared to the soft blue dress covering the knees of the Mormon sister. Are they judging me as much as I'm judging myself?

* * *

Our team is touring Snow Canyon with a geologist who will tell us all about the rock formations and the prehistoric effects of the volcanoes in this area. I'm traveling light with my white sneakers, navy sweatshirt tied at my waist and the red drawstring sack from registration with cords that fit over my shoulders. In it are wallet, comb, lipstick, cell phone, ID badge and water bottle. Four of my teammates are waiting at the Dixie Center at ten A.M. We pile in the van and, for a time, loneliness subsides. There are three vehicles which caravan, stopping at places for observations and explanations of geological features before heading to Snow Canyon.

"The volcanic debris seen along the tops of the hillsides was originally flowing through a riverbed. The area surrounding eroded away for millions of years until the riverbed and flat area far below became an inverted topography," says our guide.

I'm wondering what Lisa's husband is thinking when he asks, "How can they know how old that lava is?" I know they are religious, and perhaps they believe the earth is only several thousand years old. The explanation assures us, but who knows what it takes to convince a 'believer'?

"This pit of broken pumice results from a lava tunnel hardening while its contents flowed through and collapsing as the shell couldn't sustain the weight. Rather than enormous craters being formed by a huge eruption, this area has volcanic seams which bubbled up, hardened and bubbled up further along the seam." Our geologist is a member of one of the older men's teams, retired for many years. For several hours I am mesmerized by his vast knowledge of this topic. Ben loved things like this. I don't reach for the necklace, but I'm subdued on the way back.

Sitting next to me in the back of the van is Adele from Texas, whom I have played against many times. She is my height, and I guess one would say we were rival players on opposing teams in the older women's division.

"I didn't know you were here this year until I saw y'all last night at the social," she drawls. With a face collapsed into a complex set of wrinkles, her white hair and square features perch via a thick neck on broad shoulders. Her breasts sag over a paunch disguised by a black fanny pack hanging in front of a pair of long beige belted shorts. "I wanted to tell you I thought you looked fat in that red dress you wore," she says, critically looking me over.

"Gee Adele, thanks for sharing that. Most people would say nothing, and I would make the mistake of wearing it again." She thinks she has done me a favor. I won't bother telling her I'm back to my high school weight. I didn't notice her, or what she was wearing, because she never made it to the dance floor. But I don't say that either.

In a slow speech with drawn out vowels, she asks, "What team are you with? I didn't recognize the ladies at y'all's table." Her thin lips curl quizzically, but my eyes trail to the stubble on her chin.

I reply, "I'm playing down, Classics fifty-five. I got picked up on team finder. How's your team doing? Are you playing sixty-fives?" I have dodged a bullet getting on the regeneration program. She epitomizes what I'm trying to avoid. I smile.

"Now, yah. I'll probably medal and next session I'm doing seventies," she drawls. "Lordy be, that's what you're up to this year, isn't it girl? Are you sitting out a lot with your fifty-five team?"

"No actually, I only sat out one game. I'm playing middle but we have a great libero. I don't see a lot of back-row action. The pace is fast and our team skilled. I'm enjoying it." Perhaps I'll share my news with her. It can't hurt and the ride is long. "I'm part of a study with Harvard University Genetic Research on Aging. I'm taking supplements, which reverse my aging. In six weeks I grow a year younger. Now my Life Span age is about sixty-three."

"Come own, girl! Can't you see how evil that is?" Adele's face wrenches with terror. "It's best to not mess with God's plan. We are born, we grow old, and we die so we can reunite with our Lord and our ancestors. Can y'all imagine what would happen to society if all had your wacko ideas?"

"Yes, I imagine we will have a much smaller draw on the medical system if people are healthy into old age. I guess we will have a productive, experienced work force so we won't have to rely on immigration to provide that for us." Proud of my decision to rejuvenate, I sit up straight beside her. "Personally, I look forward to avoiding the diseases of aging and the physical affects to my appearance." I remove my sunglasses so she can see that I am looking younger.

"Don't pitch a fit; I'm just picking with you," Adele smiles her crooked smile. She leans closer and the gossip oozes slowly toward me. "Someone's bin tested for takin' drugs. You tellin' 'bout your supplements reminds me. Some people will do anything to win." Then she booms, causing me to jump, "I will come and watch y'all play so I can see how well y'all fit in with that team."

My team captain, Jodi, looks around quizzically from her seat in front.

"Check our schedule. Classics fifty-five. See you tomorrow." When we arrive at my drop-off spot, I cringe to think she will come to our court. I probably will sit on the bench. I hate to lose to her, even if it's about whether I get floor time.

"We're at the Dixie Center tomorrow. We don't have to play until ten o'clock. See you on court seven," says Jodi as I climb down from the Van.

"See you there," I shout back. I wonder if Adele heard that and if I'll get to play, now that the double elimination matches are starting — now that my team knows how old I am. What a loser! I lost Ben's necklace, I lost my position on the team, and I lost my dignity last night. Remembering my mother's posture admonition, I force back my shoulders and walk into the crowded lobby.

Three of the players I recognize from the German Global Cup team are towering over two young ladies in black yoga pants and bright crop tops, a blond and one dark curly-haired. A German, towering tall and straight as a spruce, turns on his heels and smiles as I approach slightly sun burned and disheveled. "Duh party is room seven on duh second floor. Please come do," he says.

I can't resist smiling and say, "I'm a mess and haven't had lunch."

"It's okay, ve have food and lots to drink — and music." He pretends to close dance. The girls giggle.

"Two O seven," I repeat. "Got it."

I head for 320, hop in the shower and shampoo my hair. In the mirror, I watch the naked blond blowing out her cute bob. I see her youthful curves and nearly smooth pussy. My leg, underarm, and pubic hair have not yet grown thick. I wonder if they will. I resemble a woman in her fifties, though. With that thought in mind, I toss on a long green dress which shows my figure to advantage and head for 207. Carol said to enjoy myself and take some risks. No sense missing an outing for a pity party of my own. Volleyball parties are always such fun. It's almost like I'm watching myself have this adventure. The woman in the mirror disconnects with my reality. Am I a lonely seventy-year-old or a cougar party girl?

The metal latch holds the door ajar, and music invites me in. The only food I see are taco chips and cheese puffs. I shouldn't have junk food, but carbs are a friend I know midst the strangers who fill the room. A couple is on one of the queen beds; at the desk, a giggling girl perches on the lap of a huge player sitting in a tiny desk chair. Hans, who invited me, offers me a beer and a place on the bed beside him. Asking to use the washroom, I pour the beer down the sink and refill with water. I wash my hands, grab a handful of cheese puffs and sit on the bed. Hans, an appropriate name for this guy, rests his size-fourteen Nikki sneakers on the bed while his big mitts reach for me. I playfully feed him cheese puffs as a diversion. They won't last long; I must do something else. Conversation?

"I watched your game against Italy," I intone, testing his English.

"They did not good. We are too strong, I think," says my German giant.

"Yes, I hope I see you play the US team. That game will be better," I enunciate.

"What is your occupation in Germany?" I notice his hands are moving my way. On the other bed his comrade is getting to second base with the frizzy-haired girl. His hand is inside her yoga pants. I'm glad I'm wearing a long dress, only my sandals visible beside the big sneakers.

"I make houses. Construction. It is hard work. I am soon too old for the lifting," he says.

"You look strong when you play volleyball," I keep him

talking, but get to see his muscles as he flexes for me. I will be no match for this guy with the enormous feet and big powerful hands if he decides he too wants second base, or more.

The girl on the lap has a credit card and is snorting a strip of white powder at the desk. Her partner's hand wraps around her waist and disappears under her abbreviated tee shirt. Drugs, booze, and sex. Let me see? Not quite what I'm needing right now. A panic builds within my chest. My head is spinning with the realization that my impulsiveness is, once again, leading to disaster. Have I learned nothing from the previous two evenings?

"I'm out of here. This is not for me," I say, jumping to my feet, grabbing another handful of cheese puffs, shoving the door and heading down the hall. I feel dirty and vulnerable, but not submissive. I escaped with my life, but I'm not empty-handed. I finish my diet-cheat as I wait for the elevator door to open. My mascara smudges on my hand. I pull my door key from my bra where I carry it when I have no purse or pockets and quickly let myself in, relieved to see there is no one following.

A hot tub will wash off this self-loathing. Why do I attract slime? Are younger guys all out for an easy lay? Do they not respect women? Being attractive might be worse than being invisible. My dry bathing suit hangs on the hook in the bathroom — pink body, purple shoulder straps. I need the water now, even if the chlorine is strong. I change, grab a towel from the front desk and head out back to the pool area.

The sun sinking toward the mauve hills still gives off some heat. Thoughts of rainy Seattle weather contrast, and I'm lucky to be here at this desert hotel. Three long-legged sunbathers on lounges barely glance up as I climb down the ladder at the deep end and allow six laps of freestyle to wash away the previous encounter. At least I poured out the beer and escaped when I saw what those jerks had in mind. I've been to team parties before, which involved a lot of beer, trash talk and laughter. Sex and drugs with the Huntsman games are a first for me. Perhaps social fun has changed since I was here last! Will all guys treat me as a sex object now I act and appear younger? Is that what women endure now?

No one is in the hot tub when I emerge from swimming. With the jets set for fifteen minutes, I settle in the chlorinated warmth and close my eyes. All that has gone wrong haunts me: my captain sitting me out in a tough match, getting tested for taking drugs, my team treating me like an old woman, not seeing Russell again, Tom the loser lover, Al the adulterer, Hans the German jerk, Adele's blunt truth, and losing the butterfly necklace from my beloved Ben.

Someone lowers in beside me and interrupts my ten minutes of solitude.

"I've been hoping to see you again," says Russ in his baritone greeting.

My heart skips a beat.

"There's something for you in my room." There is a touch of humor around his mouth and near his eyes.

Oh no! Not him, too. I thought he was better than that. I've been longing to see him since we first met. I'm drawn to him — his body, the way he is on the court, his humor, even his voice sends my heart into a turmoil. But if he wants to lure me to his room for some quick action, he's no better than the others. Was Ben the only decent man? Russ seems perfect for me, but not if he is trying to seduce me like those other scum.

I guess he can see that I'm not excited about going to his

room and he adds quickly, "No, not like that. I have something for you in my room. Come with me, I'll get it."

With hesitation I follow, though it seems natural to be walking with him — both wrapped in towels, leaving a path of wet footprints. He opens the gate for me and turns left to an outside door which he opens with his key. That's why he disappeared when he was following me last time! He is on the first floor. He doesn't go to the lounge area or the lobby. He enters by the side door and his room is across the hall, 133.

"Wait here," he says and disappears inside.

Probably wants to tidy up before asking me in. But he returns right away.

"I was at reception getting cookies — they make the best chocolate chip cookies here each afternoon — and I saw this lying on the desk. Someone had turned it in. I recognized it was yours — from the hot tub. I remembered you holding it and knew it was important to you. The guy at the desk said I could return it, but I haven't seen you until now." My butterfly chain dangles from his fingers.

This is too much. I gulp hard; hot tears slip down my cheeks. The floodgates of my emotions burst open. With all I've been going through, with everything beating me down to a worthless blob, I sob with relief.

"Whoa, tell me what's happening with you." Russ puts his comforting arm around me and leads me into his room. He offers me a chair while he leans forward from a seat on the corner of the king-sized bed. "I knew you would appreciate the return of your necklace, but what's with all the emotions?"

It all comes out in a tsunami: Ben's death after years of cancer, his anniversary gift, how I am reinventing myself, my weight loss, how I don't fit in with my team, and several scary encounters with men at the Games — all of it. I even explain the drug test. Why am I comfortable telling him when we are strangers? I have told no one about myself. He wraps me in his arms and holds me for about forever. In the minutes we spend together, the tension dissolves from my towel-wrapped body. His compassion envelopes me. His muscular chest is a haven for my struggling consciousness. This is where I belong.

Finally, he says, "Go, shower, and meet in the lobby in fifteen. I know an Asian restaurant that I'm taking you to."

He doesn't ask. He sends me out and I'm walking on a cloud. I'm not alone anymore. I obey, and the shower washes away my concerns. Telling him has freed me of the pain. It is like he is carrying my burden for me. My suit drips its chlorination into the tub from the grab bar. Quickly, I towel and dry my hair. My butterfly chain hangs in the scooped neckline of my white t-shirt, pulled over my lace bra and panties which top dark cargo capris, white belt and sneakers. My eyes are still puffy, but some make-up camouflages my distress. I'm in the lobby in twelve. He's already there, scrumptious in a pair of tan jeans and a form-fitting baby-blue V-necked sweater that makes his smiling eyes sparkle. He takes my hand naturally and we walk a block to a hole-in-the-wall restaurant, Ahi's Taste of Asia. We order off the wall menu and fill our sodas and waters from the machine. It's perfect. I can enjoy a carb-free meal. There are no athletes, only locals. We are alone together without the loud bustling crowd found in most places during the Games.

"Why haven't I seen you until today? And what is your last name?" I ask.

"Vickers — I'm Russell Vickers." He extends his hand and smiles. I give it a brief squeeze.

"Jeni Taylor, pleased to make your acquaintance." I return the smile and let him continue.

"We had our games at the high school and evening matches when the social was going on. This morning the guys got up early and hiked at Zion. Amazing topography!" he says. "There were several climbers suspended on the summit. The hiking is challenging enough. We did Angels Landing and the views are amazing. It's high above the valley with sheer drop offs all around. Apparently five died falling off; but not today — none of my group," Russ laughs.

"It is great here. I miss the coast though: snowy mountains, moist air, evergreen forests," I say.

"This might be an interesting change for a few months a year, though," Russ says. "How about September to November? Tell me about your make-over program: the diet, the fasting and age reversal program. It would be fun to do together. I would like to be fifty again; this time with you."

Whoa. This man knows what he wants. Or is this is his player move? "Forty-five forever has an energizing ring to it," I say and tell him about the mother who started her periods again.

"Hmmm, you want children someday?" We both laugh and he takes my hand across the table. "I want to know you better."

Why is there a pang of guilt when he mentions having children? Did I do such a terrible parenting job? My daughter and I are not close? I wish I knew why. I was always travelling with my teams and working full time. When I was at home, the house and yard took a lot of attention. More than my son, Gord, it bothered Darlene. If I could be a young Mom again, I'd parent differently. I want to tell Russ my thoughts, but he'd think badly of me.

A lovely Asian girl brings our dinners to the table, interrupting our conversation. As we eat, he wraps his leg around mine. His eyes reach deep within me, distracting me with affection and lustful thoughts. An electrical surge from his leg to mine connects us throughout the meal. This longing is something I haven't known since my courting days with Ben. Thinking of both of them at the same time fills me with peace, not guilt. Strangely, it seems I have known this man for a lifetime. With every word, he cements into my soul, filling with warmth and safety.

The full harvest moon is high in the sky as we walk back to the Fairfield. "Don't leave me alone," I think as we walk back to my room, but realize I've said it aloud.

"I can only stay for a while; we both compete in the morning. We play at ten. When's yours?" he asks.

"Ten," I reply, and he follows me in.

We climb on the bed and prop the pillows to watch TV. I search the programs on the remote.

"There is something I need to tell you about myself, Jeni," Russ says, combing his hand slowly through his rumpled hair.

"Sounds ominous." But I realize this is serious for him. "Okay, I told you mine, now you tell me yours." I turn off the TV.

"I separated when my wife of twenty-eight years told me she was a lesbian and had found her soul mate, a woman."

"Well, at least you aren't a married man," I say flippantly, "and I'm a single lady."

His usual masculine sense of forceful certainty softens as the burden of sorrow he carries surfaces. Drawing his gaze to the closed curtains, his shoulders slump heavy into the pillows. The pause, as he gathers his thoughts, intrigues me and I give him the time he needs.

"It's just that, since she left," he continues, "I haven't been with a woman. Well, I've been with women, but I guess my performance level sucks. I can't disappoint you; I'm telling you up front — not to expect, well, you know — a performance."

He's crushed. This is hard for him to say. It's my turn to hold him and dry his tears. Not the outright sobs he saw from me, but my heart breaks for him.

"I'm not after your body, as delicious as it is. I appreciate your affection and companionship. It is comfortable to be together." I curl up with my head on his chest and my arm wrapped around his waist.

"Wake up, Sweetie. It's eleven o'clock," whispers Russ. "We both fell asleep."

Impossible! I could never fall asleep with a man besides Ben. Russ kisses me gently on the lips and disappears out of the room.

"Breakfast at seven," I hear as the door shuts.

"OMG," I text Carol. "It's Russ! Dets to follow." I pull on my cozy PJs and get ready for bed.

CHAPTER 9

When he's near the sun comes out.
"I'm alive," I want to shout.
Treasure found to guide my way,
As I love and laugh and play.

Having breakfast with Russ makes waking up early worthwhile. My sports bra and uniform are clean and ready, my knee pads dried out on the air conditioner. I take my supplements with a glass of tap water. My face is rosy from yesterday's hike, so mascara and pink lip stain are all that's required. I double check my backpack, dump in my wallet, water bottle, and ID from yesterday's sack with a zip-lock bag for my carry-out lunch. Russ waits, sipping coffee. We go through the breakfast line together, piling on the proteins, fats and fruit. He laughs when I pack my zip-lock bag, but wraps some in a napkin for himself. The TV in the dining room blares a Huntsman Games' update — a story of drug testing in the sport of volleyball. It shows footage of a women's game but doesn't name me. A red flush colors my face, but Russ wraps his arm around my shoulders as we leave the dining room behind.

* * *

The Classics are warming up for our last pool play match. I'm relieved to be playing middle again. Tammy is back in her libero shirt. She wanted to play all around. Fair enough. I am the newbie and it only makes sense that I should sit. I was being hormonal, but now the world is beautiful, and I love my teammates and I love Russell. Yes, I think I do. I touch my butterfly chain and know that it is right to be with Russ. In fact, I sense Ben made me lose the chain, so Russ could recover it for me. I see Russ warming up on his court, passing and laughing with his buddy.

"Hey, you passing or only looking girlfriend?" says Julie, dragging me back to the task at hand.

"I'm looking and passing," I say, tossing her my ball. "I have to talk to Jodi. Be right back."

"Jodi, can we talk?"

She nods and we sit together on the team chairs as the rest warm up. "I had to do a drug test. Possibly someone mistook my supplements, which are making me younger, for performance-enhancing drugs. I wanted you to know because the team might suffer."

"I already knew about the test. I saw you talking to Alice during the game you sat out. I asked about it. They will not kick you out or penalize our team."

"But I saw it on the news and everything."

"Forget it. Let's play ball." Jodi joins the team and I wave at Julie who is waiting for me.

We win two in a row, which means we don't work the

next match. As I'm picking up my gear from the bench, Adele shows up.

"I watched your second game. I reckon playing with outstanding players sure 'nuff makes you play better than I remember." Adele gives one of her back-handed compliments. "I could probably find a team that needs a hitter in this division too, but I can't do that. What would my team do without me?" She runs her hand through her short grey hair as slowly as she speaks. "I think players should really play in their own age division, not one that's three divisions younger. How are the older ladies going to have a good level of competition if the stronger seventy-year-olds move down to play with the fifty-fives?"

"You've got a point there, Adele." I gather my gear together. "They really need you on the Texas Stars."

I see Kate on the bench with her back to us, taking this all in. As she passes me, she rests her hand on my shoulder. What did she mean by that? Was she telling me she has known all along that I am seventy? Was she agreeing with Adele? I shouldn't think I fit on a team like this? Was she laughing at me? Or was it a gesture of support — agreeing with me that Adele could never fit in with any team except the Texas Stars.

Since we tie Roof for first place, both will play weaker teams in the first round later this morning with the next hour off. Russ' team, also destined for the finals, plays two courts away. Our first matches are against two of the weakest teams, though also in the Gold divisions. From this pool play, the top eight teams play in the Gold Division. The next eight play in a double elimination tournament also, but it's the Silver Division. The remaining teams are in the Bronze. This means that, even though our opponents are weaker teams, they are among the top eight of the age division. All games will be fierce competitions.

Since my match has finished quickly, I sit for the end of Russell's last pool play. He's only in the front row but gets to serve before the libero replaces him. He serves four points in a row and plays back row that whole time. His team runs a five-one, which means one player sets in all rotations; therefore, only five players can hit. Poor passing requires the setter to run after errant balls. Russ' passing is on the money. I can see why he loves playing back row.

Adele, who also has a break, settles her butt on the chair next to me. "Who you watchin'?" She has to know everybody's business.

"My boyfriend is the middle blocker on this side," I say, trying to keep the grin from showing.

"You can't be serious! You've got to be twenty years olda than him! What could he want with a woman your age? You could be his mother." Her face is pale with astonishment. "You think some crazy ideas, Jeni."

"I suppose he wants what any wonderful man wants — love and affection," I smile sweetly.

They win in two games. His team avoids work assignments to give us both an hour off. He takes my hand, in front of his teammates, in front of Adele too, and with backpacks over opposing shoulders, we walk out of the gym.

Upstairs there are some upholstered benches and Russ leads me past the massage rooms to the far end. I pull out my water bottle and zip-lock bag.

"I didn't come here to eat," Russ says, "I need to talk to you." He takes my face in his hands as I sit at his side. My bag and lunch drop to the bench.

"I don't know what this is all about," he says seriously,

"But I want you to know that I care about you. You're all I can think about and it's all unbelievable."

I lean into him and close my eyes. His lips meet mine and part slightly, not passionately, but lovingly. His sweaty jersey is moving sensuously against mine. He smells of clean musk, testosterone and pheromones. "I know this is too soon, and too soon after Ben's death perhaps, but I need you to know how I feel."

I glance down at my necklace and say, "Ben wants me to be happy. You recovering my chain was a message from him. You are the one. You make me happy."

"Why do I make you happy, Jeni? We hardly know each other?" Russ looks adorable, his lips firm and sensual.

"Well, that look for one thing. I'm only kidding. It's much more than how you look; it is how you make me feel: complete, protected, excited and calm all at the same time. You are compassionate, non-judgmental, competitive, caring. All of this makes you attractive. You are sexy too," I laugh.

When our lips meet again, it is with passion. The heat rising in both of us. He pulls away in amazement. "What are you doing to me, Jeni?" he says.

"Let's finish our matches; then find out?" I say laughing and we head back to the courts.

"Where did you get off to?" asks my captain, but doesn't wait for an answer. She is busy filling in the line-up sheet. They already flipped for service, which we won. I grab a ball and pass it to her when she finishes. Her sets, high and accurate, make my passes and my hits controlled. When we are ready to spike, I take the ball to the left front position and toss it to her. She sets me high and outside. I usually like a "three" which is midway to center, but right now I'm flying high. I approach from the ten-foot line, whip my arms back, jump off both feet and meet the ball with concentrated force, driving it down the line.

"Nice hit," says Lisa. "You will replace me as strong-side hitter if I'm not on my toes."

It occurs to me that we are playing Roof. Their warm-up balls are pounding on our side just as hard. This will be an important match, sending the loser to the consolation side with the slight hope of returning to play for the gold medal.

I'm starting at middle, between Lisa and Carol. After the practice of pool play, my timing and spacing work with both players who position solidly, taking away the line while I block the cross-court shot. I learn where each is likely to hit; some like the line, some hit hard cross court and some like to dink. With my mind clear, my focus is on winning. If I think of Russ, I mimic his playing — smooth, agile, powerful. It helps.

After the first win, our captain, Jodi, says at the bench, "Jeni, you're playing great today, and it's a big part of our win."

Wow, I didn't realize I was playing any better than usual! "Thanks Jodi, I'm glad we won, now let's keep the momentum going."

We jump out to a five-point lead but lose it when their big hitters rotate to the front and I'm still in left back. Their six-foot-two hitter pounds one past Julie to the middle of the court. I dive, sliding my hand under the spot where it is about to land. The ball bounces upward off my hard-pressed hand, allowing Tammy to bump set for our strong-side hitter who puts it away down the line. I'm happy I'm wearing knee pads because my dive is not as smooth as those who had coaching in high school. My teammates high-five me. I beam.

"Way to go, Jeni." I hear a familiar voice at the sideline.

Russ has finished before me and is cheering us on. Roof's fans wedge him in, but that doesn't stop him from yelling encouragement to us.

After that, our team surges ahead, winning the second game by four points; sending Roof into the consolation bracket.

As the girls gather their possessions from the bench, I run to my man, throw my arms around his neck and he swings me around, our sweat mingling together. Our teams are in the two o'clock finals for the gold medals. The worst outcome is silver. If the team returning from the consolation wins the finals, they play another game. Double elimination means all teams except the champions lose twice.

"Impressive pancake," he says, referring to my diving save.

"Thanks, I guess I enjoy back row too."

"Time to pull out the lunch bag," he says. "Can I split a salad to go with our eggs and fruit?"

I grab my backpack, hoodie, and his hand. We make our way through the courts to the concession stand in the hall. We order blue cheese dressing and sit quietly with our heads almost touching to avoid scattering salad on the table. I can't imagine anywhere I would rather be. Russ spreads my sweatshirt over my shoulders, so I won't get chilled. His hands linger, smoothing wrinkles from the navy fleece, sending warmth flooding through my body. I want to run my hands over his wet jersey, and over his shorts, his face, and his hair. I struggle to keep my hands to myself and as he reads my thoughts he smiles, one of his eye-crescent, dimple studded smiles. I laugh and smooth the hoodie over his shoulders instead.

"Don't need this. I'm not the least chilly now," I say, casually spreading out the wrinkles on his shoulders, letting my hands relish the touching as long as I can without drawing attention.

"Get a room," calls Jodi from the concession line. I guess we are being obvious. We stifle our laughter, quickly stuff the remains of the salad in our mouths and toss the trash. Russ picks up his stuff and I follow him outside to a warm shady spot on the concrete benches.

"In an hour, we need to get to our teams. We can't let what's happening between us, distract from our games. It's important that we both win — it's important to our teams for us to focus," he says.

"Let's get these medals won. What do you mean, 'What's happening between us'? What is happening?" I ask.

"That's what I will find out. I'm having such a hard time keeping my hands off you. You are so damn beautiful. So desirable," Russ says. "Is it only a physical attraction? I'm sexually drawn to you but, more than that, I want to protect you. I want to be important to you."

The Utah desert air dries our hair and uniforms. We ignore the fact that our knee pads are still up. I always pull them down right away. That's usually the first action when I come off the court, but I've had someone on my mind. Russ has ignored his too, and he sat through the entire last half of my game and also through lunch. He uncovers my chain, tucked beneath my jersey collar, and tenderly holds the gold butterfly. He lifts my chin, asks permission with his eyes, leans in, and presses his moist lips on mine. Eyes closed, my heart races and I grasp him closer with my hand on his neck. Russ draws back.

"It's complicated. I don't know if I can let myself enjoy you. What if I have too much baggage? You deserve a complete man," he says.

"It's you I'm wanting; and not only for sex. I am safe and

fulfilled when I'm with you. Is it more than the Games' experience with its exhilarating energy? I want this to last. I need it to grow into the best life can offer, not a fling," I say. "Is that what you want?"

"More than I can express. Let's talk after the finals." He takes my hand as silently we walk back through the lobby and into the noisy gym filled with twelve courts of competition. He leaves me watching the game where Roof is finishing their opponent. It is no surprise that we will meet them at two o'clock. I watch him disappear into the crowd which has gathered to see the men's final. The women enjoy a solid fan base, but not as many as the younger men who play a faster, stronger match. The thought hits me. Russ is much younger than me. I find him attractive and am flattered that he likes me, but is it realistic to consider of a future with him? I remember Adel's words. His mother could be younger than me! What does he expect of a woman my age? What if my age reversal program does not keep making me younger? What if I soon turn into one of the frumpy, gray-haired ladies with no waistline and sagging breasts? Will he still want me? I see the tall, beautiful, athletic women on my team who prepare for the finals.

Focus! I belong with this group of women. At least it seems like I fit in here. As I sit for the last points of the consolation final, breathing deeply I run through the tapping and affirmations of Emotional Freedom Technique, preparing myself mentally for the most important game of the tournament.

CHAPTER 10

Doing what I love to do
I'm a winner, through and through.
When my love can share with me,
There's nowhere else I'd rather be.

'm starting at middle-blocker, matching up against Roof's towering blond. Jodi, our captain and main setter, is running a 6-2 offense, setting first from the back row. We win the first service and she puts one over the net down the right side. After a nice pass to their setter who predictably sets the power hitter, I slide to the right, shoulder to shoulder with Sandi, cutting off the cross-court path while she takes away the line. We go up in unison, fingers spread above the net, and send the ball to the floor at our opponent's feet. A superb way to start a game! We win two more points before turning it over to the opposition, but soon get it back. Sandi is serving while I'm switching back to middle with Kate, the second setter, acting as weak-side hitter. She's not as talented a blocker as Sandi, but her vertical amazes me. She's only five-foot-six and gets well above the net to deflect the hit. And when Jodi gives her a back-set, she is ready to attack and scores in the far diagonal corner. Our team is on fire.

A sizeable crowd gathers for finals in each division; not bleachers as there are on court one, but chairs two-deep around the perimeter of the court with fans standing beyond that. It can get noisy, especially if the match contains a team from South America. There are no Brazilian teams in our division this year. Brazil is consistently in the last match. They are amazing.

You shouldn't peak too soon, and we've saved it up for this final. Roof is exhausted after coming through the consolation bracket. They finished a close match. It hardly seems fair to put them up against us without a break. But we will gratefully take any advantage we can.

We came to win, and we do — two games straight. I don't get another pancake, but get points hitting out of the middle, and three nice blocks. My serving isn't awesome, with one in the net and one long during the two games, but decent. Tammy comes in for me across the back row, which I don't mind because we are running smoothly. What matters is the victory, not me proving my ability. I remember a coach saying, "It's okay to lose; just don't do it on my team." I'm not the only one who puts winning right up there with being debt-free or stepping down a dress size.

When the last whistle declares the game over, our team runs into a huddle and gives three cheers for Roof, and shakes their hands as we meet at the net. We will see them again on the podium as they get the silver and we go home with gold medals around our necks. Now if I had my credit card paid off.

The noise from the men's crowd shows it is not over on court one. We must pass by them on our way to the presentations in the lobby. With my bag slung on my shoulder, I guzzle my water. Russ is on the court, his team down eight to six in the third game. The men are swapping sides at eight points. He sees me signal that we won our division and sends me one of his heart-melting smiles. I want to stay and watch the end, but my teammates hurry me out. I hear a great cheer, and know they won the next point. Now I'm in the crowded lobby, the doors shutting out the noise of the competitions.

Alice Malot, tournament director, walks toward me. "Jeni, I'm glad I caught you. Your tests came back negative, which you undoubtedly realized since we allowed you to continue playing. However," she frowns up at me, "if you come back in the seventies, we will test for the substances you said you are taking. It is obviously an unfair advantage." She turns her back and stomps off.

The sixty-five plus women's teams are being presented with their medals. I recognize Adele, winning bronze, and others from many years of competing in my age division. With my smart phone, I snap several players I remember. Barbara Jones who organizes the top team rushes over.

"Jeni, I didn't know you were here. Who are you playing with? You look amazing. I love your short hair and haven't you lost weight or something?" She's pumped from their win.

"Hi Barb. I'm with Chicago Classics. We won the fifty-five-plus division over Roof. Thanks and congrats on your win. I'm on an age reversal program. It's really working," I say, pumped too. Like, why must I tell everyone my secret? It comes tumbling out. I assume they want to know. Why wouldn't they?

"It sure is. Email me about it — kinda busy gathering uniforms now," she says stuffing a shirt she's been holding into her bag.

It is a challenge, after a tournament, to get the photos and collect the uniforms. They are gathered sweaty because it's easier to launder them at home than have them mailed from all over the country. Too often players forget to bring a clean shirt, rush off for engraving, forget and drive away wearing their uniform, or hurry back into the gym to watch a friend play their final.

Let's get finished so I can see Russ play. The bronze and silver winners from the fifty-fives are already on the stand. The center podium is empty. They call my name. I bow my head and receive a red-white-and-blue ribbon with a heavy gold medal, slid on by a high-energy Jeff Probst type who shakes a hand or, in my case, kisses a cheek. I take my place among Classics and beam convincingly for the photographer. Jumping down from the stand, I pull my Huntsman Game t-shirt out of my bag, rip off my uniform, and replace it with the dry blue tee. I don't notice that, in Mormon country, stripping to your sports bra is immodest. I toss the hot pink to my captain, who smiles and nods toward court one.

"We'll talk later. Impressive job. Now get in there and support your man," she says.

"Thanks coach," I shout over my shoulder as I hurry away.

Russ' team is one point ahead fifteen to fourteen. The third game, to fifteen points, must be won by two. It is game point and Russ is serving. Remembering my two missed serves, I hold my breath. The referee signals for him to serve. He lines up the valve on the ball, tosses and powerfully drives it over the net. You can see the ball wobble as the receiver struggles to pass it to the right front position. His setter barely gets to it, and the hitter adjusts to his inside set, resulting in a free ball deep in Russ' corner. He takes it with his hands and sets directly to the power-hitter, who pounds through the blockers to score the winning point. I go wild. It's as exciting as when we won our own gold. They give a brief cheer and slap hands with the opponents.

Now Russ is grabbing his bag and heading my way. Sweat is dripping from his face onto the chest of his drenched white singlet. What a fine-looking man! A smile reaches across his face with those alluring dimples on each end of a row of pearly white teeth. Scuffled curly hair matches the light gray peeking from his jersey neckline. He throws down his bag and, with his arms around my waist, lifts and twirls me. There's no hiding our affection.

I squeal with delight, knowing he is claiming me with our teammates watching. Hand in hand we move to stand near the Podium, our blissful gaze interrupted by the calling of his name. He ducks down for the diminutive lady who is making the presentations now. When he gives her a kiss on the cheek, she blushes. My cell phone snaps a dozen pictures of him and his team cheering and laughing, medals dangling.

"Let's get them engraved," I say when he returns, "but first, hand in the jersey."

He dutifully tugs it over his head. His arms up reveal a body that I can hardly resist throwing myself toward. I imagine the eyes of every woman in the foyer riveted on this sweat-covered specimen, but I can't take my eyes off him to check if it's true. He replaces it with a gray sweatshirt, zipping it halfway up the front. His eyes meet mine and he knows what I'm thinking. I blush and lead him down the hall to an engraver who will get them ready in half an hour.

The team name, year of the tournament and the division are the usual lines of engraving. When they get thrown in a box with dozens of others, it's the only way to identify their origin. I like to take masking tape and write on the first names of the players. Then I can remember who contributed to this win. We pay and wander to the nearby benches.

"Do you want to check out the Gift Shop? There are some stylish shirts this year," I ask, hoping he refuses.

"I have all I want, right here," he says, bringing my hand to his lips.

"Your medal?" I joke. "Russ," my tone becoming serious, "I told you why I am falling for you, but what do you see in me?"

"Hmm, let me see. You are pretty. I like that. But you are very complex. First, you are sexy and fun-loving. You are trusting and vulnerable. You are funny and intelligent. You have a kick-ass competitive side that I adore. You take your health and conditioning seriously. I want to wrap myself around you and protect you from any more hurt. I like who I am when you're around."

I snuggle in beside him and we enjoy the physical exhaustion of the day. Contentment settles over me and life stills. This moment could continue forever. The joy and fatigue of victory, combined with the sweet euphoria of Russ, create the perfect experience.

"They're ready," I say eventually. "Shall we shower and have dinner?"

Hanging the medals around our necks, Russ holds the door as we head across the street to the Fairfield. It's still hot out and we both sweat easily. "Definitely time for a shower," he says as we enter the lobby, automatically grabbing for the same chocolate macadamia nut cookie. He gives it to me and takes a chocolate chip for himself.

"Pick out what you want to wear to dinner tonight, but don't shower until I get there," he says heading to his room. I get on the elevator. As the door silently closes, I grasp his meaning. He intends us to shower together. I'm embarrassed and excited.

What would Carol think? I haven't told Carol about this. I haven't called her since the second day. What kind of friend am I? She worries about me — we always share. I must call her tonight.

I reach my room, leave the door ajar with the metal bar, tidy up the sink and select a blue cotton shift with a low V-neck. There is time to set out my bra and panties — the door pushes open.

"May I come in?" asks the familiar deep voice. His arms are full as he backs into the room.

"It looks like there is more than the entrance planned," I laugh.

He tosses his jeans and a teal cotton shirt on a chair. I notice flip flops and black cotton briefs and his DOB kit. He unzips the hoodie all the way to his navel. "I plan to shower with you, to lather your entire body, if I may."

I pull the drapes shut, check that the door is closed, and saunter up to the man standing half-naked in my hotel room. Why the hell not? I hear Carol's words in my head. "We DO need to shower. We are in the desert, so let's conserve water," I say, looking innocent. He laughs.

His arms wrap around my waist, and he kisses my neck. "Salty," is all he says, and continues to pull my t-shirt over my head. Black sports bra, black spandex shorts press against black cotton shorts and a naked man-chest. His lips find mine and, with eyes closed to enjoy the moment, he staggers me into the bathroom. He steps out of his shorts and I struggle to release my breasts from my wet bra and drop it on the floor. His hands press down on the waist of my shorts and takes my panties off at the same time.

"Let me look at you. You are incredibly sexy," he says.

I'm grateful to have found the program to gain my lost years. There is no way a gorgeous young Russell would look at me a year ago. I know I appear ten years younger and my body is trim and firm. My shape and energy compare to the young person I remember. Preparation for the Huntsman Games has toned my tummy, my thighs, and my buttocks. My muff is no longer concealed by curly black hair. A silky light patch reveals my swelling labia. He seems to find this attractive so; I shrug off my inhibitions, grab my shampoo and step into the shower.

The initial shock of chilly water is invigorating. Russ steps in behind me and starts soaping my back while I lower my head into the warming stream and shampoo my hair. It should be twice as fast to shower with two people on cleaning duty, but he is finding places to wash that I usually ignore. He is extremely thorough. The entire bathroom is steamy when I turn to wash his sterling physique. I start with his hair, his chest, his arms, his legs, his back — I can be thorough too. I wash his privates, though I think he might protest, remembering what he said about having self-doubts in that arena. His penis is large but hangs only semi-erect. I lather him gently with my hands, pressing myself against him, and kissing him tenderly as I rub against his reluctant shaft.

"It's okay," I say. It is comforting to enjoy this play time. "If you are happy, I am." We rinse, dry, and silently dress; me at the sink and him by the desk. It only takes minutes to dry my hair and pop on some mascara and lip gloss. I check in the mirror before revealing myself to him. My mouth drops open when I see the man who shared my shower. The teal shirt is perfect for his eyes, fitting his broad shoulders and tucking into a form fitting pair of dark denim jeans. Flip-flops protect tanned, bare feet; his smile melts my heart.

"Wow," we laugh in unison.

CHAPTER 11

For many years, I've felt no stir.
And he had doubts because of her.
Now is the time for us to see.
Awake my sexuality!

The Rib and Chop House, right across the street from the Fairfield, has about twenty people waiting outside; but Russ made reservations while I was drying my hair. They seat us in the far back corner, which is relatively quiet. By reading lips and sitting close, you can even enjoy a conversation.

Tonight athletes from both sessions are in town and want to eat out. The Classics 50 team sits out on the patio with only two replacements to my fifty-five roster. I leave Russ to order for us and go to chat with my teammates.

"I was hoping I'd see you before I head out in the morning," I say to Jodi bending close to her because of the noise. "What a precious experience this was for me. After being away from playing for a few years, I've come alive again."

Their food has arrived and cutlery clatters midst the

raucous conversation of players celebrating and catching up with teammates. Tammy is sitting next to her.

"You earned the medal. Thanks for playing with us," my captain says. "I checked your registration and didn't realize that you are seventy. That's amazing! No wonder they thought you were doping. I hope I'm playing as well when I'm a senior."

"I can send you my regeneration regime. It's from the latest research that comes from Harvard Genetic studies. Age is a treatable disease. I'll email you some stuff. It sure is paying off for me. I never would keep up with you guys without it."

"Deal," she says.

"Send it to all of us. You're proof it works," says Tammy, who has been listening in. "I heard that you were seventy before we began. I kept watching to see if it was true. You were proving the rumor wrong, girl."

"I'll send it for sure and thanks," I say. "Kick ass in the next session too. I've got to run. Russ is ordering for us."

Their eyes follow me to the table in the back where the total stud is waiting anxiously, smiling as I return.

A tall glass of orange juice and ginger ale sits at my place. He's remembered that I don't drink alcohol but wants me to celebrate with a drink other than water. I take the eight ounces of water first because I'll suffer muscle cramps if I dehydrate. Following a full day of playing is when I'm most apt to get them — badly.

"Don't you hate getting muscle cramps after playing?" he says, like he's reading my mind. "I always take salt or some kind of electrolyte drink to avoid it."

"Me too. Too much in common," I laugh as I lean in close so he can hear what I'm saying. "Tell me about yourself. I know I love you; the chemistry is amazing, but more than that, my spirit is at peace when it's near you. I am complete. But there is much I don't know. Are you still married? Do you have kids? Are you retired? What do you do besides volleyball?"

"Wait a minute. Lots of questions. I have the same for you! Let's alternate," he says. "First, I'm still married but the papers are ready to file. The separation is simple with an equal division of assets. She has an apartment with her girlfriend. The house is up for sale. Your turn."

I set down my glass and prepare to unveil the truth. "My husband died two years ago, and I still live in our house, but it is over-sized for one person. Grown children: son married, no kids, living in Australia; daughter has two kids in Bellingham. She and her husband are both teachers. They were here for Ben's funeral. It was wonderful to have them all together, even if it was a devastatingly sad occasion."

Russ interrupts, "We had no children. Beth said she couldn't get pregnant, but I thought perhaps she didn't want them and preferred an alternative relationship. Turns out I was right," his smile disappears, and I want to hold him.

The cute blond waitress turns up with our entrees: medium rare steaks with Béarnaise sauce, asparagus and Cole slaw, substituted for the potatoes.

"Perfect," I say, amazed that he knew how to order a carb-free dinner. I wait until he starts and when his mouth is full, I ask, "So are you retired?"

He almost chokes and grins, "Perfect timing. I'm working off and on."

Oh great, I picked one who's a flake.

"My company designs and produces decorative signs for Parks and Recreation: State, Regional and Federal parks mostly, but some commissioned out of country. I work about two days a week and my guys do most of the traveling and overseeing our projects. I like that I can work from home. How about you?"

I move the food around on my plate. My life is mundane compared to that! "I retired from working in a pharmacy five years ago. I put my life on hold during Ben's illness. For the last year and a half, my job has been rebuilding my life," I say wanting to keep no secrets.

"Tell me about your journey. I like the results, but I want to know how you got here," Russ says with genuine interest. We are eating slower than I'm used to. I normally finished by now, but I guess this is how eats properly, enjoying each bite and the conversation too.

I gaze into those concerned eyes, "I felt drained, old, overweight, unattractive and alone when Ben died. Old age was creeping in — fatigue, lack of ambition, sore weakened muscles, and aching joints. To get back my lost years and overcome depression, I returned to Volleyball, putting my name on Team Finder. A team of strangers, fifteen years younger than myself, picked me up." I search for the age difference to register. For him to do the math.

Seeing no concern or rejection, I continue, "I work out with my girlfriend Carol. You would love her; well, I do. We go to the gym most days. But the best results are from changing my diet. I can burn sugar, all carbohydrates turn into sugar, or I can burn Ketones." I'm babbling again. Stop it, you fool, or you'll drive him away. "I love the foods: avocado, fatty meats, eggs, butter, whipped cream, berries, vegetables, cheese and nuts. What's not to like?" Oh no! I can't stop! "Also there's intermittent fasting which encourages autophagy."

"What's that?" he asks. I can't believe he's wanting more information. Most people reach their limit by now.

"The cell searches for food and since I'm fasting, it

cleans up junk in the cell: viruses, old dead bits. It turns them into amino acids for building cells. The fasting let me lose weight, nearly thirty pounds, and because my diet contains lots of fat, I don't get hungry the same as if I was eating carbs," I say looking up sheepishly to see if he's still listening.

"Okay, but that's only healthy living. I know lots of people who fast and restrict their eating — vegan, vegetarian, whatever. You're doing something else, right?" he says.

Here comes the hard part. Is he going to get up and leave me without finishing his meal? He knows I'm older than him, but I don't think he's aware how much older. Will it turn him away? Will I suddenly become invisible? God, I'll hate losing him. Go ahead. Pull off the Band-Aid, Jeni!

"I'm seventy years old, Russ. That's fourteen years older than you, but I have the drive and stamina of late fifties." Confusion clouds his features. Here it comes. This is where he leaves.

"You're joking, right?" he says in disbelief.

Say something, Jeni. "I'm not kidding, Russ. The regeneration regime that I'm following makes me a year younger in six weeks. It won't be long before I'm younger than you," I laugh, hoping to make light of the issue.

His smile vanishes, wiped away by astonishment. Suddenly his face becomes grim. "Why didn't you tell me sooner? Like in the hot tub the first night? Is this a lie you've kept from your team too? Can't you see how I've been deceived?" He rips out words as his eyes harden.

"I couldn't tell you that night. I was attracted to you and couldn't believe you were interested in me. Why would I throw in something that might ruin it?" Tears leak out as my heart breaks. Gathering my dignity, I respond sharply. "And

I was right. As soon as you find out my age, you are angry. It's a deal breaker, I know."

"Hold it, Jeni. I'm not angry because you are older than me. I'm angry because of the deception. My wife kept stuff from me throughout our marriage and it devastated me. I can't have you deceiving me. Does your team know?"

"The captain saw my birthdate when I registered. But she acted like it made no difference to her. I know that a player from the sixty-five division told Tammy, the other setter. She kept looking at me, waiting for me to screw up. She mentioned nothing either. I played as well as the rest of our team," I say, hoping that if I am played well, he will accept me too.

His face softens. "I understand why you didn't tell me. Actually, if you had, I would have thought you were trying to get rid of me. I admire what you have done. To make yourself young again and prove it on the volleyball court is fantastic. If I can learn from you and play like I did twenty years ago, I will be grateful."

Now I'm a case study for his benefit! Well, at least he isn't angry anymore.

"How does it work? What do you do?" he asks unbelievably curious about my regime. Expressions of confusion and anger replaced by a focused fascination.

"Aging is a disease. It is the degrading of the epigenetic layer of the DNA." I try to keep the wavering emotions out of my voice. "That's the regulating layer that determines what the cell is — muscle, blood, hair and so on. As I'm getting older, more of that layer needs fixing, but the sirtuins and NADs can only do so much."

"The what?" Russ says.

"Sirtuins and NADs are the repair crew. Rather than

YOUNG

allowing damaged cells to replicate, they fix the epigenetic layer." I ask cautiously, "Is this too much?"

He shakes his head. "No, I want to understand. Complex maybe, but if it's the fountain of youth, I want to know about it," he says.

"By taking NAD enhancers in the form of specific supplements, I produce more sirtuins and NADs allowing the epigenetic layer to repair. Then the cell can replicate as intended, not become one that's confused and damaged."

Russ bites his lip and frowns. "Are there side effects from taking this?"

"Yes, there are side effects — all good. For example, the mitochondria in the cells produce the energy for this process and I make more of them, which gives me piles of energy."

"Where do I get these supplements?" The napkin has slipped off his lap, and he retrieves it from the floor.

"I'll show you in our room," I say. "They're in the fridge." Why did I say 'our room'? I suppose I am used to having teammates share the room. It came out automatically.

He's finishes his meal and I still have some left on my plate. That's not like me. I'm usually the first one finished. This is a habit I developed when my kids were small. I would finish dinner and go for a mile run. When I got back, the family done, I could clean up.

Obviously, I was talking too much. He thinks I'm a motor-mouth — an old motor-mouth.

"OK, you can show me — when we get back to 'our room'," he grins. Not much gets past him. I like that.

"Shall we split a dessert?" he asks.

"I'm good," I say. My appetite has diminished with anxiety from his anger. He calls for the check.

I take out my credit card and his hand rests on mine. "My treat," he says.

"Don't you want to be my Toy-Boy," I laugh, still dwelling on our discussion, "kept by an older woman?"

He looks hurt suddenly, "Don't even joke about it. We are equals, but it's my treat this time." The smile is back.

It's dark when we leave with the full moon riding on the crest of the hillside. Walking together, as equals, seems right. He takes my hand and leads me through the crowd still waiting to get into the restaurant. Can you be equal when one always leads? Hmmm.

In minutes we are in the hall opening the door to 'our room'.

"What time do you play tomorrow?" I ask.

"Ten, at the Dixie Center, but I need to register first. When is your ride coming for the shuttle?"

"Nine. I'd like to pack tonight, then I can relax at breakfast before I leave. Would you like to meet for breakfast?" I say.

"No," he says. I'm confused. "I won't meet you for breakfast because I'm staying the night and we will go down together. Okay?" he says.

Oh my God, it actually is 'our room'.

My heart is pounding as I'm caught off balance. A flush rises in my cheeks. I've never spent the night with a man besides Ben. A man will be sleeping in my bed, touching me in the night. "Okay," I say.

I go about packing my suitcase. Marie Kondo would be proud. Except for my laundry, zipped in the bag's bottom, my clothes are folded, rolled and placed side by side in my gray carry-on. I drape the ones I intend to wear in the morning on the chair: jeans, a long-sleeved white turtleneck and my red denim jacket, comfortable for traveling, yet warm enough for a Seattle arrival. With my gray pajama bottoms and white tank top over my arm, I head for the bathroom. Russ props on the bed, amusing himself with the remote, channel surfing through program-interrupted commercials. At home I only watch streaming television networks: Netflix or Crave or Prime. It is strange to hear how entertaining commercials are and how often they interrupt a show.

"I'll set the alarm for seven, okay?" he says.

My mind is racing as I calmly wash my face, apply moisture cream, brush my hair and teeth, and tidy my toiletries for an efficient exit tomorrow. From the fridge, I take the two jars containing my molecules and scramble up beside him.

"Talking continues," I say, dressed now in my comfy jammies. "These are the supplements." I give a brief explanation and hold up the second bottle. "That's all there is to it. Voila, a year younger in six weeks. I order them over the Internet. Expensive though. Like buying new volleyball sneakers each month for this program, but it beats the alternative. I've been there."

I pop them back in the fridge and perch on the end of the bed. "Now I ask you a question. Are you dating since you separated?"

"When I explain that I can't — well, perform in bed — that is enough to scare away most women who consider I'll be a fun ride. But there is a girl back home who ignores it. Marie, she's a hot babe in her early forties. She says she'll make me come around because she wants my babies. Her biological clock is ticking. She tries to seduce me with her big breasts and booty."

I scoot up on the bed beside him. "Do you want to give her your babies?"

"I've always thought I would make an excellent father," he says, a faraway look in his eyes.

"All I want is to be close to you. I can't seem to get close enough." I wrap my arm and leg around his body to distract him, and he turns toward me. "Enough about the other women. This is about us," I say.

Russ takes my leg off him and sits up.

He's changed his mind. I was stupid to dredge up thoughts of women who want him.

He pulls his shirt over his head, unzips his jeans and throws them both on the chair with my prepared morning outfit. Dressed only in his black briefs, he turns off the lights, except the one beside the bed, and throws back the covers.

"My tournament starts in the morning. I need a sound night's sleep," he says, "and I want it to be with you. I want to wake up with you in my arms in the morning and our hair all messed up. Morning breath — the complete shit."

"I haven't slept with anyone since my marriage," I confess. "I don't know if I can."

"Well, I don't know if I can do any more than sleep, so we're even," he laughs.

I throw back the duvet and curl up beside him. He reaches over and turns off the bedside light.

He whispers in my ear as his lips linger on my neck. "It's still early. I thought I might enjoy touching you for a while."

My libido, which has been mostly dormant for years, suddenly perks up its saucy head. I draw in a shallow breath and hold it, letting the sensation flow over me. I can't appear anxious or demanding. I turn towards him and share a deep lingering kiss.

"Tonight is for exploring you, pleasing you. Don't worry about me," he says.

"I don't want intercourse tonight. I won't make any request but that," I say. "Usually men only want sex. Well, I want all the rest."

That's obviously the right response. The pressure comes off him. In the dark, a tear falls on my shoulder.

His exploration begins at my neck, makes its way down my muscular shoulder and across my collarbone. His hand moves up under my top and his fingers circle my breast, first the right and then the left. My erect nipples cry out for touching. He slides down beside me, stretches my white t-shirt up and turns me toward him. He takes the left breast in his mouth while rubbing the nipple of the right with his left hand, causing sensual vaginal tugs as my labia swell. My back involuntarily arches.

His hand leaves my breast and finds its way to my waist. He releases the tie on my bottoms and slips his hand beneath the fabric. Tiny nibbles at my breast followed by a gentle sucking sustain my arousal as he reaches for my warm moist area. I part my legs slightly allowing him to thrust deep inside finding lubrication for his caress. My swollen clitoris waits anxiously for him to return and pay it the attention for which it yearns. He spreads moisture in the area and strokes lightly, sensing my excitement mount. Suddenly he stops sucking, stroking... WTF?

He will not leave me hanging! Will he? Maybe since he can't climax, he's showing me what that's like.

Once again, too quickly I jump to conclusions. He throws back the covers, pulls off my bottoms and goes down. He nuzzles between my legs, indulging in the musky aroma, and licks open my labia to find my throbbing clit. Kissing, sucking and flicking with his tongue. He is masterful. He is dominant. He... he's... driving me over the edge. His fingers drive deep inside me in time for the powerful contractions of my climax.

"Oh, my God. That's was amazing," I pant, covering my mouth as I yawn. Russ scoots up beside me and his arm wraps around my waist.

"It was good for me too," he says. "Could I lay on top of you for a minute? I miss that part."

My arms open wide and he climbs over me with our private parts touching through the cloth of his briefs. As I kiss him, he stirs, but I'm ready to sleep. Perhaps later. He rolls off, curls around as I lie on my side, and this is how we sleep.

CHAPTER 12

To love and lose is that my fate?
Will I now lose another mate?
Should I be glad to know that he
Took this time to flirt with me?

*M*y bladder wakes me an hour before the alarm. Hairbrush and mouthwash interrupt my trip back to bed. Russ lies curled toward me, but there is room for me to slide in, facing him. He is too delicious to resist. His shoulders uncovered, I move in close, put my leg over his waist, my arm over his shoulder. I kiss him awake. His morning erection stands stiff beneath his briefs, and his kiss is passionate.

"Good morning," I say.

"I thought I was dreaming," he says as he becomes fully conscious. His shaft is still threatening to find its way home. My pajama bottoms lie on the floor.

"It's only a few minutes after six," I say. "I couldn't resist waking you." I remove my leg and let him get out of bed. He looks down at his shorts, tented in front.

"It's only a dream," I say. "Pay it no mind." He walks into the bathroom to relieve himself and wash his hands. When he returns, his bulging briefs are flat in front.

"Let's not get up for half an hour," he says while I pull him down beside me.

"I get to explore," I say. I crawl on top of him, fitting myself directly on his crotch. I pull my top over my head and toss it on the clothes pile. My breasts bob shamelessly in his gaze. His hands move from my waist to adore my breasts. Warmth spreads from my genitals to his, causing his cock to bundle beneath me. I lower my head to kiss and nibble, and my hand rests on his pecks. I notice his nipples are erect too. I tweak him gently and then firmly. There seems to be a direct connection to his penis. When I tweak, there is action down below. I slide off and move between his legs, pulling off the briefs to release his semi-aroused shaft. My hands wander down his thighs and up the insides, cradling his balls. I glance up to see his eyes closed and a longing smile encouraging me to continue. I take the tip of his penis into my mouth, running my tongue around the circumference. As I grip the shaft, his hips thrust his penis into my mouth and he is fully erect. I let him stroke several times, reach for his nipple and pinch while I climb aboard, sensing him deep inside. He rolls me over and my legs automatically wrap around his waist with my hips elevated for full penetration. I guide his thrusting action so I can stay with him as his pace increases. With a cry, he comes. The warmth of his fluid floods inside me. He rolls off, and tears pour down his cheeks: tears of relief, tears of gratitude, and tears of love. I stuff his discarded briefs between my legs to prevent a spill on the bedding and curl up at his side. His arm wraps around under the pillow to reach my breast on the left. As he squeezes gently, his right hand slides between my legs. His fingers find the moist nest and finish what he started. It's quick because I am incredibly aroused by this man. He strokes lightly, and within minutes I shudder delightfully and hug him as if I never want to let him go.

"I'm sorry, Jeni. I never thought in a million years I would meet you and that we would make love. I didn't have any condoms. I didn't even think about it until now." Russ searches my eyes for forgiveness.

"Well, I don't have to worry about getting pregnant." I pull his arm around me and sink into the pillow.

"Bringgggg," startles us and Russ reaches over to touch the alarm switch on his phone. The end of our night together; the start of his next tournament; the beginning of my journey back to reality; the end of our relationship.

Quietly, I dress while Russ jumps in the shower and shaves. "Like a married couple getting ready for a work-day," I say. The thought of our coming separation spreads shadows over my earlier bliss.

"But I usually wear underwear on work days," he laughs, pulling his jeans over his naked butt and stuffing his shorts in his pocket. With my turn in front of the mirror, I fix my make-up and hair. My medal hangs around my neck. Traditionally we wear medals travelling home. They spend the rest of their existence in a shoe box on a top shelf. I take my supplements and tuck them with my pajamas and toiletry bag into my backpack. A quick check of all the drawers; a tip for the maid; we are ready to roll.

The dining room packs with people checking out and teams preparing for the morning games. I slide my bags behind the reception desk and, with my handbag slung over my shoulder, join Russ in the food line. He's piling sausages, eggs and fruit on his plate. I place two glasses of water on the only free table, claiming it. He nods and drops off his plate while gathering cutlery and extra food for lunch. In the zip-lock bag I hand him, he conceals the bagel, cream cheese, jam, strawberries and hard-boiled eggs which will see him through until dinner.

"I've learned so much from you," he says, a grin from ear to ear.

"Quiet and replenish your fluids," I say, grinning back.

We are oblivious to the rest of the crowd, leaving only briefly to grab more food.

"How is your team going to do this session," I ask.

"It will be hard to top last week — not only the medal I'm talking about," he says. "The team is from my hometown. We aren't as strong comparatively, even though we're in an older division. I'm the most experienced of the team and a lot of the pressure will rest with me."

"Next year I will play two sessions as well and we can go to the socials together," I say not wanting to talk about leaving.

Fox news is playing on the TV over our table. The Battle of the Buckeye State — Ohio is having the Democratic primary debates.

"Nothing on the impeachment hearings? It's all over the other channels. Fox news can't handle the truth," Russ says, finishing the last of his breakfast. On this we agree.

Eventually he realizes the time to leave has come. "I'll go get changed and meet you at the entrance." All I see is his back as he heads down the hall.

I drag myself to the front desk, retrieve my bags and check out. My ride will be here in ten minutes. People rush by, to the gym, to the parking lot.

I don't give a damn where they're going. My insides are ripped out and I will cry at any moment. What if he doesn't make it here before my ride comes? Is that how we leave it?

My hand brushes my butterfly necklace and I think of what we might have had together. He would fill the hole in my life. I don't know his contact information and he doesn't know mine. I ask for pen and paper at the desk and write my name, phone number, email, and address in case he makes it back before I go. He must!

I move my suitcase and backpack outside near the planters where the car will pick me up. The sun is shining. How dare it? Rain would be more fitting. It rains in cold Seattle. I'm out of place here.

I am almost in tears when the door opens and Russ is there, a sports bag with sneakers tied on the handle. He's in playing shorts with his knee pads around his ankles. His water bottle is empty. I'm warm again. "I wrote this out for you," I say, "in case you want to contact me."

Russ smiles and puts the paper folded in the zippered pocket of his bag. "I didn't want to take the time to fill my water and leave you waiting," he says. "I'll fill it at the gym after I register." He notices my puffy eyes and hugs me tight. "Don't worry, I'll see you again soon."

As my ride arrives, he kisses me passionately, looks deeply into my eyes, pushes me back and registers a long full length gaze before hugging me again. "I want to keep that in my memory until I see you again."

"Thank you for letting me feel love again, Russ," I say.

"Thank you for letting me feel again, Jeni," he says. "I *do* love you."

The driver loads my bags; Russ holds the door for me and as we pull away, he heads for the Dixie Center and Session Two.

The Huntsman Games van takes me to the shuttle depot a half hour before my bus leaves for Las Vegas. Time enough to phone Carol and make sure she meets my flight in Seattle. I check the time of arrival and call.

"Well, about time," Carol answers, seeing my name on her display. "I've been plenty worried about the trouble you've been in without me to take care of you."

"I've fallen in love, Carol," I say.

"Oh sure, it's been almost five days. I'm sure this will last," she scoffs.

"I've got to tell you all about him. He's amazing," I say, trying to convey the seriousness of my emotions.

"You know I want to hear all about your adventure and I'm glad you know it's time to move on," she continues. "Is he a divorcee or old widower?"

"It's Russ. He's young, fifty-six; semi-retired lives in Portland. He has a girlfriend there, but he loves ME," I say.

"Okay, time for a reality check. I don't mean to burst your bubble, but I'm your BFF. It's you and I, the two single ladies, remember?" she says.

I don't like this conversation. "My flight comes in at five to six. Are you picking me up? Departure drop-off at Alaska, where you dropped me off. There will be less traffic there. Okay?" I say changing the subject.

"Sure, I'll pick you up at six and we'll go somewhere for a bite to eat," she says. "See you."

In the back of the bus, I stretch out with my tablet connected to the Wi-Fi, but I can't focus on my on-line video games. Carol's words race through my head: adventure, five days, reality check, single ladies. She's probably right. She usually is. How can someone find a life partner and believe it's the right one in five days? There are things about Russell I don't know. I don't even know his contact information. Probably he'll lose mine or will think better of this experience when he gets back home to his alluring tiny forty-year-old girlfriend. Well, I did him the favor of getting him past his impotence. He can go back to Portland and make her babies. He should be happy with someone who lets him be a father, someone who's petite and beautiful... not an old, infertile, amazon like me. If he's with her, he can stay in his own city and marry someone he's proud to show off to his friends. She must love him if she wants to have his babies.

Life at the Games is artificial; none of the actual struggles of home. It's a make-believe world, and we are characters who fall in love, and it has nothing to do with our proper lives back home. I should be grateful that I had this taste of love and youth. Lots of people my age dream of having a young, handsome man become infatuated with them — to hear him say that they are beautiful and desirable. How can I be so gullible as to believe it means more than what it was, a fling, and an imaginary romance?

Carol has been my rock through Ben's illness, through his passing, through my rehabilitation. She has supported me in my wild dream to go back to volleyball while I pretend that I'm fifty-five. She has helped me pick out my wardrobe for my slimmer body. She listened to my failed encounters with admirers and laughed with me at all the risks I've taken. She's the one who will be there for me when I get back to Seattle and let the memory of Russ fade into the story I share with her.

I turn to my tablet and a tear falls on the screen as the shuttle crosses the city line. At the Las Vegas airport, another fantasy bubble presents. Lines of slot machines flash their enticement on the way to my gate. I wouldn't dream of putting money into them because I only bet on a sure thing. Like Russ. That's a stupid thought. Why say he's a sure thing?

I pick up some trail mix and water to keep me distracted

on the flight. My head fills with his memory: the sight of him shaving, his tanned feet in flip-flops, and the sensation of his hands on my body, the satisfaction of our lovemaking, him going up to block at the net, listening intensely as I tell of my age reversal program, his acceptance of my age, his obvious love for me. I run through my cell phone photos of his team receiving their gold medals and crop several of my darling. My heart swelling with these images, I get on the plane, smiling all the way to my seat. I toss my carry-on in the overhead compartment and stuff the backpack under the seat in front of me.

CHAPTER 13

Head home. Huge house.
Friend fills the gaps.
Still hang to hope, as if a rope,
That he will call, perhaps.

"What's the medal for?" A stocky middle-aged lady, seated in the middle, asks.

I didn't realize it was dangling back and forth as I walked and now, as I slipped my bag under the front seat, was banging on her leg. "Sorry," I say. "We must wear them home from a tournament. It's tradition."

"Tell me about the tournament. What sport?" she wants to know.

I settle in beside Fran and explain the Huntsman World Games, getting picked up by a younger team, my dead husband, my latest boyfriend, the amazing rejuvenation possibilities — everything. For someone who was tight-lipped about my age for the last week, I now am proud of my age. Russ' acceptance has made me accept it too.

I learn about Fran too. Her divorce, her kids that no

longer speak to her, her recent retirement, depression about not being attractive in the dating field. We are both surprised by our need to share with a complete stranger but do not maintain a connection.

The rest of the flight I fantasize about my night with Russ, enjoying the calm of knowing I am safe and loved, wanting it to stay fresh in my mind. But as the flight nears the northwest coast of Washington, my thoughts darken.

Carol is waiting, and she will not encourage my fantasy. She will want me to return to the life we know together where she is my most important friend. While I was with Russ, I never called her — didn't even come to mind. Perhaps that's why she sounded disparaging of my love. She's jealous that he would take her best friend away. I've been selfish and neglectful.

While Ben was ill, I treasured the times I had with Carol. Our revitalized friendship is important to us both. After our work-outs at the gym and pool, we'd sit in the hot tub and talk about our high school days. We'd relive a childhood without worries or responsibilities. As teenagers, with me she escaped the turmoil of her dysfunctional family. Her mother, a bi-polar, and father, an alcoholic, made our relationship and sports especially important to her. She escaped into a teenage marriage to get away from the conflict too, hoping for a less stressful home. But that didn't work out. Her solitary life now seems idyllic and carefree because it is what she chooses. Now, is she wanting to escape her solitary life to be with me?

With Ben's death, each moment we spent together made my loss bearable. She helped me plan the funeral. Carol was a help with my make-over regime, coaching and encouraging during the entire program. She held me accountable and celebrated my successes with me. She shopped with me. She helped clean out Ben's clothes and tools, tasks I found difficult. We scourged my pantry of carbohydrates and sugars. I am her pet project. Her life revolves more and more around me.

I see our relationship is evolving again, and Carol is afraid it won't include her. I must let her know how much she means to me and how grateful I am for her friendship and support. My next trip might be with her. I smile. She can keep reins on my promiscuous behavior and prevent me from throwing my heart into the abyss. Or we'll be promiscuous and throw our hearts into chaos together, I laugh. She might see the success I'm having with my nutrition and age reversal programs and want to get on board with that, too. But only if it makes her happy. I don't love her less because she now appears and seams older than me. She is fun and has great energy. I know her savings aren't as comfortable as mine, but if she reset her priorities, she could afford the molecules too. She spends on that beater of a car. I will be more respective of her Mazda. That beater picks me up in ten minutes.

Checking my cell phone, which has reset to Pacific Standard Time, I remember that Russ has finished his first two games with his fifty-five team. What is his next team called? Vintage fifty-five? I'll check the results on-line when I get home. He may call to tell me how they did. I'm smiling again as I pull my carry-on out of the overhead baggage area and hoist my backpack on my shoulder.

There are several planes arriving with hundreds of passengers heading for the baggage carousels. My luggage is a carry-on so I head directly to the Arrival drop-off at Alaska Air where Carol will pick me up, avoiding all the congestion at the lower level. Leaving the terminal, I breathe in the fresh moist air of the coast, chilly compared to the desert climate of Utah. I secure the front snaps on my red jacket, which is hardly warm enough for west coast fall weather. The squeal of Carol's brakes announces her arrival. When she pops the trunk of her 2001 Mazda, I throw in my bags and slam it shut.

"It's good to have you back," Carol says as I lower myself and buckle up. "Not much has happened here compared to your last week."

The radio is playing Maroon 5's, *Memories*. She reaches to change the station because she remembers it made me sad. The song is about memories of our lost loves, but now it sounds like the most beautiful song. My memories of Ben and of Russ blend seamlessly to give me joy. I am blessed. Lucky to have known love and marriage, and now lucky to love a man who accepts me unconditionally.

"Your team did well. I followed on the website. How did you play? I want to hear all about it," Carol says as she pulls into traffic.

"It was wonderful, knowing I can play well with women fifteen years younger. Most of the players did not know I am seventy-years-old. The molecules are entirely worth the money. I cheated sometimes on the carb restriction, but mostly I was careful. I didn't fast at all because Monday was a playing day, and I didn't want to risk running out of gas. It wouldn't be fair to my team. They were encouraging, young and athletic. Most had recently turned fifty-five. I'm sorry I didn't call to tell you about it, but I got distracted," I say, Russ filling my mind as the ultimate distraction.

"Tell me about your affair," she says, "Was it unusually hot? It made such an impact?"

"It has been only a few days, but it seems right. It will help me move on. I am desirable and loved, whether or not it lasts. He should probably go home to the gorgeous woman who wants to raise his babies. Eventually, he'd tire of his friends commenting that I could be his mom. But now I know I can find love again. I wasn't sure of that before. This is the first time since Ben died I've thought about a future with another man. But Russ might not even call me again," I say discouraging myself with negativity.

"Or perhaps he will," Carol says optimistically. "Until then, where shall we eat?"

"You choose." Interesting that when I am negative, Carol automatically turns positive to cheer me up. My response results in Carol driving directly to a place nearby on International Boulevard, Chontong Thai Cuisine. She planned this all along. This choice allows us to miss the heavy downtown traffic. I hear the brakes with each deceleration.

"Sounds like the brake pads need work," I say to a grunt response from Carol. We leave the gray skies and drizzle outside and our eyes adjust to the oppressive black and flowers as we snake to a small table near the back. An old Asian woman takes our order and brings a plate of Pad Ka Pow with beef for me. Carol has Pad Thai because she knows what she will be getting. Mine is delicious and I leave only a bit of rice. I drink three glasses of water, which amuses the old lady. As soon as she fills my glass, I empty it.

"Any plans?" Carol asks as we leave after paying the bill.

"Laundry," I laugh. "I'm taking it easy tomorrow." I am only planning to check how Russ' team is doing and wait for his call. "I can't tell you how much I appreciate your friendship — picking me up at the airport, having dinner with me, and the rest."

"I appreciate your friendship too," she says.

"I foresee my next trip will be with you. Where would you like to go?" I ask as we leave the parking lot.

"Oh! Somewhere warm but not too expensive; I'll consider it," she says. Traffic is slugging smoothly, and it is only a few minutes before we stop at my Capitol Hill home.

"Call me tomorrow and we'll see what mischief we can get into," I say as I retrieve my bags and trek up the path to a green three-storied house with a wide veranda. All the homes in this neighborhood are at least a hundred years old, and all remodeled, keeping the exterior of early twentieth century. The boulevard lines with light-barked deciduous trees. The falling leaves remind me of one simple chore for tomorrow.

I see the Mazda pull slowly around the corner at the end of the block. Why did I imagine her life as ideal? She is living all alone, like me. When I open this door, no one is there to welcome me home. There is no one to laugh with or even watch TV with. No one to share my bed or my shower. I throw my keys in my purse and drop it on the hall table with the pile of mail from the floor under the mail slot. Up the massive staircase to the master bedroom, I carry my bags, hoisting them onto the high king-sized bed. I fill a basket from the walk-in closet with my laundry items. My other clothes, I hang in the closet. Sneakers find a spot on my shoe rack and I smile thinking of the court adventure they enjoyed. Slinging the empty suitcase onto my closet top shelf seems to symbolize the closing of a chapter in my life. It was only a trip. There were many sports trips and will be more. Why is this one different?

The deep claw-foot tub is filling with hot, bubbly water while I start the laundry cycle, downstairs. Passing my office off the kitchen, I power up my computer. "When I finish my bath, I'll check Russ' team's results for the day," I say aloud, clutching the mail from the hall table.

My bathroom is steamy with lavender fragrances. White

candles lit on the stand replace the overhead glare and dance silhouettes on the nine-foot ceilings. Adding a cup of Epsom salts from the enormous jar under my sink to ease my sore muscles, I step into the bubbles. Only my head and knees are above the water, I realize it's great to be home. No one to soap my back, though. I remember the St. George shower, the games, the meals, and the lovemaking. As water cools, I revisit the days Russ and I spent together, the sincerity of his words. "Surely I will see him again," I say aloud. My revelry broken, the coolness of the tub registers. I quickly dry with the white plush towel from the wall hook and slip my plaid bathrobe over my naked body.

The pillow shams support me as I settle to read the mail. The usual bills and flyers tossed aside, a letter from the hospital calls out to me. My hands tremble as I expose a bill and accompanying letter. What??? It's been over a year since Ben's death. The bill is for one hundred and thirty-seven thousand dollars, three hundred and eleven dollars and twenty-six cents. There must be a mistake. Apparently, they used an experimental drug during Ben's treatment. We tried everything we could to save his life. The insurance company is refusing coverage during the use of this drug and were fighting a court case with the hospital for the entire cost of his care during his illness. Not only did I lose my husband, but also I may lose my home. We have never worried about financial issues, but this is more than chunk change. There were immediate expenses from Ben's passing, which depleted our joint account temporarily, but I thought I would be comfortable with dividends and pensions going forward.

Still reeling from the letter, I phone Carol.

"A hundred and thirty-eight thousand dollars?" she repeats. "Where can you get that?"

"I don't want to think about it. I can't lose our house. It's all I've got. My pensions aren't enough to afford this house. But I'll think of something. I must." I can sense Carol's sympathy. She has known financial stress all her life, but for me this is something new.

Downstairs in my office, my thoughts of Russ distract me from my dilemma. I search Advancedeventsystem.com which shows sports event schedules and results, choose Huntsman World Games, and scroll through events and divisions until I come to Men's Fifty-Five Volleyball. From a list of all teams in that division, I click on Vintage Fifty-Five. It shows two wins and a loss for his team.

This tournament will be difficult. Vintage is his home-town team. At least he has his friends around him. I wonder if he has flip-flopped back and forth as I have; alternating between living with me and loving his independent life in Portland with the fertile forty-year-old. Did it interfere with his ability to focus? Did it tire him having sex before play-ing? I've heard that guys lose some of their stamina; that it's best to abstain the day of competition. He could resent me not leaving him alone this morning. I'll ask him when he phones.

The clock reads nine or ten in St. George. Russ will be heading to bed because his games start at eight in the morn-ing. His team probably went out for dinner and he has better plans than go to his room and call me. I'll bet he wants to cut it off abruptly rather than to give me false hopes.

I get ready for bed and as I turn off the light I say, "Good night, my darling. I'm grateful for your love." I'm saying it to both Ben and Russ. In my heart, I want to believe there is still hope for us. Dark thoughts of the debt replace the comfort of love and deny sleep despite my exhaustion.

CHAPTER 14

Boundaries required. This is my life.
You are my friend and not my wife.
We are a team, facing the weather.
Life could be better if we're together.

*C*arol drops by, walking in without knocking, to find me sorting my laundry on my bed. She folds and puts clothes away with me. "Well, did he call?" she asks.

"No," is all I say. The dull ache in my heart is not visible.

"Okay, who needs a man to ensure a brilliant life? Take me. No man, no care," she says. "Women nowadays are complete with friendships. Our libidos wane, and that's fine because hormones get us into trouble. Women live longer than men — therefore women get to do whatever they want with the best years of their lives without having to take care of some guy. You are a strong, beautiful, independent woman who can enjoy lots of male partners — or female partners if you like. Russ is doing you a favor — waking you up to your potential and letting you choose your own life. You still have me; always will, Jeni."

"He will call. I know it, Carol," I wipe my face on a towel from the clean pile of laundry.

"What's on the agenda for today?" She changes the subject. "Are you going job hunting?

"First this laundry needs putting away; I'll fix some breakfast and want to get out and rake leaves in the front," I say. I realize that her life revolves around me. When did she switch over; change from friend to companion?

"I'll finish with the laundry and you go fix your breakfast. We'll rake leaves together," she says.

"There must be business on your list too," I say. "Or we could go to your apartment and do your stuff?"

"Nope, whatever you decide is fine with me. We can get some sushi and go dancing tonight — or a movie," she says.

In the kitchen, I think about my relationship with Carol. It would be easy to invite her to move in here. Her rent could help with my cash flow. Ben's side of the closet is bare. We get along well. But is that what I want for my life? I wish Russ would call. If I share my life with anyone, I want it to be him. I scoop out an avocado, which has softened during my absence. Breakfast materializes automatically, but I get distracted.

"You know there are a lot of empty drawers I noticed when I was putting laundry away," Carol says. "This place is bigger than you need for one person."

Is she hinting that I should invite her? Two old crones sharing a house on the hill? Doing everything together? Treating men as entertainment to discuss and discard? Will that be a satisfying life? I possess an active libido now and will get younger each year. I want a career and perhaps young friends. Is that what she wants too? I can't talk to her about this; at least not until I hear from Russ.

I sit at the computer and pull up Russ' schedule: play at

nine, work at ten, play at eleven, and play at one in the afternoon, all at Hurricane where my Classics team played on the second day. Hopefully he filled the zip-lock bag with lunch because there is nowhere out there to buy food. I remember the double gymnasium located outside town near the shooting range and the Dinner/Dance barn, the heat of the desert sun and the sound of his voice cheering from the sidelines. I briefly check my emails. Nothing.

I search for job opportunities in pharmacy. That would bring in enough money to make payments on the medical bill. I fill out a resume template: education with dates, work experience with dates and skills. It may not require age, but the dates all show that this person is seventy years old. I can probably find a presentable photo, but the dates are a dead giveaway. Who will want to hire a seventy-year-old? I've been out of the field for long enough that everything has changed.

"I've got your breakfast on the table," Carol says. She is taking over the kitchen, preventing the bacon I deserted on the stove from burning.

My head isn't screwed on right. I need her to take care of me; to stop me from self-destructing. I sit and shovel in my breakfast, take my supplements and clean away the dishes.

We both put on our warm coats and scarves. "I'll meet you in the yard," I say, heading downstairs where I grab two rakes, two pair of leather gloves and a collapsible leaf bin. It is four steps up to the back yard where the fruit trees are almost covering the lawn with their leaves. "No, not here. Let's do the front. No one sees it back here and there may not be enough steam to do both areas today," I say, waving my rake toward my BMW parked beside the house. There is something sad about the back yard being filled with dead discarded leaves. The branches hang deserted and discouraged. Like my life. Will it ever know what it is like to be fruitful and productive? Will I?

The boulevard looks untidy. We start at opposing ends and rake towards a pile between us. My elderly neighbour, returning from walking his dog, calls over to me, "Jeni, it's good to see you out and about." Carol drops her rake and heads across the street to pet the beagle.

"Hi Don." He and his wife lived across the street since Ben and I bought this house. "How are you and Ethyl doing?"

"Pretty well considering." He doesn't have to say more. Considering they are in their eighties. Considering all the horrible symptoms of age they and all their friends are dealing with. "You're looking well, Jeni."

"Thanks. I got back from a volleyball tournament in Utah. My team won the gold!" Don has always encouraged me to play and gives me a thumbs up. He was quite the athlete in his day. His day. Why does it stop being 'his day'? "Say hello to Ethyl for me."

"Will do." He walks up his path dragging an excited beagle.

Carol returns and says, "You have great neighbors. This is a beautiful part of Seattle. I'd love a house here."

"A thought has been bothering me." We're alone on the sidewalk. I shudder as I reluctantly continue. "Can I talk to you about it?"

"What's up?" She grins as she leans on her rake.

Anger colors my voice. "Does your life revolve around me? Are you are hinting you should move in?" My boundaries are being violated and I must clarify my position as much to myself as to her. Being the agreed upon support person is on a slippery slope to becoming a companion. No need to be angry at my best friend. Frustrated about Russ not calling and tired from the trip, I'm also upset about the hospital bill. If she paid board, it would help with my bills, but I won't let money dictate how I live. I pause for a reaction.

Her smile dissolves into dismay. "No, Jeni. I only want you to be happy. It's all I've ever wanted. I am sometimes lonely in my apartment and I know you will be lonely too in your big beautiful house, but Jeni, I don't want to take over your life," she says taking a step toward me dropping her rake, tears welling up in her eyes.

"I'm sorry. There's a lot of pressure right now. I need to learn to be on my own. I want to be in control and make my own decisions, okay?" My voice is forceful and determined. "I married young and I've never had the chance to run my life. Now is my chance. I don't want you taking over. I will always be grateful for the help through Ben's death, but I don't need that level of help now. I need some space."

The look on her face shows she is deeply hurt. She rakes to keep from crying. We'll deal with it another time. I'm sorry she's hurt, but I'm not sorry I brought the subject up. If I keep these feeling to myself, resentment will build up and ruin our friendship. I pull my attention to the leaves on the street. Cars parked along the road prevent us from cleaning off the street, but we are thorough.

"I'll get the flower beds," Carol says, picking up her tools. We must manually clean the beds along my pathway where the rake is too awkward. Her knees show wet spots from kneeling on the grass. Soon a yard-high stack centers on the sidewalk. I release the clips on the bin, and it pops into formation, ready for filling.

"Jeni, let me know if I'm being pushy or anything. I know you are becoming younger and fit. I'm afraid you'll leave me behind. I don't want to lose you again," she says, tears close to the surface.

"You'll always be my BFF. You know it," I say, walking a fine line between comforting and maintaining distance.

We take turns dumping handfuls and pressing them down and when the job is complete, move it together down the driveway to the compost bin at the back. We work well together.

"Shall we hit the market before lunch?" I say.

"I'm fine. But I'll keep you company," Carol says and waits shivering by my car while I change to my black boots with the medium heel. I grab my shopping bags and purse.

On the computer they post the results for the morning's matches. Vintage is in the Gold Division, but not the strongest team there. No emails or text messages. My head hangs as I lock the front door and run down the steps to meet my waiting friend.

"Jeni, could you follow me to the car repair shop? I want to get the brakes done, but we'll go downtown in yours."

I agree. "We go right by the place, anyway." Jim's is a shop where all of us get our cars serviced. She leaves the keys with Jim after parking by the fence. In minutes we are on our way downtown.

The Seattle market is fun to visit; not always the best prices, but the food is fresh. We can't get all the items on my list but dairy, eggs, fish, fruit and vegetables are there in plenty. Carol tries to put chocolate in my cart, but I tell her I only eat bars sweetened with Stevia or sugar alcohols because hers contain carbs. I have some at home which I promise to share so she'll know it's not a sacrifice. I love chocolate, especially dark with sea salt or milk chocolate with mint.

She helps me carry my canvas bags stuffed with almost a

hundred dollars' worth of healthy food. Our breath is visible like delicate clouds.

"I'll fix dinner if you want to stay," I offer. She nods.

"It would be better than sushi; what about the dancing?" Carol says as we circumvent the space tower on our way home.

They hold the volleyball social tonight for the second-session athletes. I wonder if Russ will go; if he will meet someone else. Perhaps he'll meet a tall middle blocker from a fifty-plus teams which is playing this session. Maybe they'll go back to the hotel together. No wonder he isn't calling me. He could be with anyone. Why would he choose me?

"Well?" Carol asks again.

"I don't feel like dancing or even going out," I say. "But you go ahead."

"Not without you, girlfriend. I need a wingman." She places the bags in the open trunk and hops into the passenger seat.

"Okay, you smooth talking devil. I'll be your wingman tonight." Who knows, it might be fun to dance. I remember the last dance with all the old athletes and country music. "Switch on the button to the right of your seat — the leather seats heat," I say and watch her delight as it warms.

"What's great about living alone? You haven't got a date when you want to go out." I ask her. "I'm not your date. You're my friend who is helping me through a tough time." I try to distance myself, but her silence tells me I've hurt her feelings. "I guess a wingman isn't a date," I say, trying to cheer her up. "After the dance you can sleep over. I'll drive if you like. The guest room is empty." It feels very different when I suggest her involvement. I don't sense pressure.

What's that all about? It is about being in control of my choices.

* * *

Carol and I giggle nervously as they smudge our wrists with red flower stamps at the door. In the bright glare of overhead lighting, the DJ plays soft rock music. I'd guess there are about a hundred middle-aged people lining the China Harbor hall. It is vaguely like the high school dances I remember from fifty years ago. Ladies are on one side of the room and men line at the bar or huddle as far from the dance floor as possible. We are definitely among the most senior members of the crowd. Carol has borrowed my white dress, clean from the laundry. I think I'll let her keep it.

Before the regular dance, which starts at nine-thirty, a West Coast Swing lesson is being taught. Since this is new, I want to take part. When Carol agrees, we get up on the ladies-line, facing the backs of fifty men who watch the instructor. On her command, they turn and walk toward us. I bet they will dance with the girl on either side, leaving me without a partner, I worry. Luckily I am chosen by a friendly male who extends his hand and introduces himself. He's shorter than me but doesn't seem to mind. We are dance partners for only a brief time, followed by a rotation as we try the steps with someone else. Soon I know some West Coast Swing, and the names of a half-dozen men. Carol and I are more comfortable as we get drinks to place on the table where we've chosen to sit. The room dims, rock music blares, and lights flash in time to the tunes.

"Jeni? I thought it was you." Harvey, Ben's friend, pulls out Carol's chair and sits beside me. Carol is off dancing with one of her partners from the lesson.

"Hi Harv. I didn't expect to see anyone I know," I say.

"I come to these dances often. It gives me a chance for some companionship without having to date. It's too soon to think of filling Iris' shoes. We loved to dance, and sometimes I imagine I'm here with her. Silly, huh?" Harvey twists his rum and coke in his hands and looks up, checking for my response.

"So you aren't dating again?" I ask.

"There are lovely ladies who would like to do more than dance, I suppose; but how can they know I want only friendship." Harvey says. "Jeni — you look amazing. Would you like to dance?"

Harvey is slightly taller than me, with short grey hair and tidy beard. I have always enjoyed his dry sense of humor. He is in better spirits tonight than he was at Ben's funeral, which is understandable because his wife and his best friend had passed away.

We nod at Carol coming off the floor as we head out. Harvey is an excellent dancer and the rest of the evening, we jive, waltz, foxtrot and even West Coast Swing. It's fun to try the moves from the lesson. I notice Carol doesn't spend much time sitting out. She doesn't need a wingman, but she shouldn't go home alone after a night like this. It might tempt one to take a ride with a stranger, like I did in St. George. I can't believe I did that.

Carol drags a chair up beside us. "Are you guys enjoying the Dog-Poop Dance?"

"Why would you say such a thing?" I ask, knowing she will have a smart answer.

"Well, ain't no big deal to break with fellow. You say, 'I break with thee; I break with thee; I break with thee' and throw dog poop on his shoes," Carol says in a clipped European accent. "Then you go down to the singles' dance and look for all the boys with dog poop on their shoes. There is a pack of dog-poopers here tonight." With a toss of her hair, she's off to the dance floor with another of the pack.

Harvey and I meet glances and burst out laughing. "That could explain the odd aroma of this place," he says. "A whiff of aftershave, perfume, deodorant, and sweat blend with some marijuana, tobacco, and booze to create the unique odor found only at single dances."

I say good night to Harvey. "That was a fun evening. I was dreading it and only came because Carol wanted company. Thanks for showing a girl a wonderful time." I extend my hand to say goodbye. Harvey takes it and presses it to his lips.

"Thank you for letting me enjoy myself. You're comfortable to be with — and a superb dancer," he says, releasing my hand. "I'll see you again soon."

Carol hands me my jacket. "What was that all about? He's the guy from Ben's funeral, isn't he?

"Let's get out of here. That's all the drama I can handle." We walk to the car silently.

Thoughts of being single and dating, even with a wingman, are frightening. Flirting and balancing relationships with men who aren't important to me, men who are being companions with benefits, makes my skin crawl. I deserve better than disposable relationships.

At home, I keep my cell phone on the sofa beside me and check often for texts and emails. Nothing. If I ask Carol to move in, I wouldn't have to be alone. This is what our nights would be like: going to the singles dances, watching Netflix together, snacking, and talking about what men we want to date. There is one man I want to date, but obviously he's not on the same page. Living with my best friend would be better than living alone. I could ask her. I loan her a pair of pajamas and hear the shower running in the hall bathroom before going to bed.

* * *

I'm up first in the morning, checking the Huntsman results and schedule. They have one last game of Pool play and in the afternoon will be in the Gold bracket. I email Barbara, the team organizer for the sixty-five team, and attach podcasts and articles about David Sinclair's age reversal program. I send the same material to all the members of the Classics fifty-fives, which I have on my group contact list.

Carol comes down in her/my pajamas. She sees what I'm doing. "It could have an interesting effect on the senior games if half the athletes are becoming younger each year, while the other half are aging normally."

"I know few who hear about this revolutionary breakthrough do what it takes to extend their lives. It's difficult for people to change the vision of who they are, or how they expect their lives to unfold. Most expect to grow old and suffer like their parents did." I know she is a doubter.

"It isn't natural to extend your life. What would happen to our pensions if people lived twice as long? Messing with cellular infrastructure is risky," she says.

"Or they don't value themselves enough to spend the money," I counter. "I know what will happen if I don't take care of business. I will soon get old and succumb to the degenerative diseases of aging. I am optimistic that my life and health will only get better as I get younger. Even if my wrinkles and graying hair continue, I will be happy if my internal organs are healthy."

Imagine what would happen if the population gets on

board. "We could ideally double the workforce by allowing healthy seniors to continue working part time or voluntarily using their experience and skills developed over the years to make us less dependent on immigration. You know, the birthrate has already dropped below the level where there are enough productive people to maintain our standard of living, let alone care for a decrepit lot of seniors."

Carol agrees, "Families in the United States don't provide care for their elderly. Most families have both parents working to even pay for their own homes, cars, clothes, entertainment, and medicine. Care homes are less than desirable places for our old loved ones."

"I'm avoiding all that. But you know, it's hard to change habits unless there is a reliable support system. I'm lucky to have you backing me up," I say to my buddy.

Carol sits disheveled at breakfast. There is no toast, no coffee. I pour ice water in two tall glasses and set them on the flowery place mats with the cutlery. Bacon, cheese and onion omelets with fresh guacamole and salsa proceed two bowls of blueberries with sky-high whipped cream.

"Looks great," she says. "Gonna miss the coffee though."

"You can grab a Starbucks when I take you home," I say inferring the stay is only temporary.

"I thought we could go by the gym today. You don't want to stiffen up. We might as well continue the fitness program, which works for us both. Can I borrow workout gear?" Carol says, assuming I'll agree to loan her some of my old exercise clothes. She may as well take them all because I'll not have need of that size again.

"I am cleaning house. Vacuum, dust, clean bathrooms, water plants — you know, it takes a lot for a house this size. You don't think a maid comes in, do you?" I laugh.

"It always looks like a maid left minutes ago," she says. "What do you want me to tackle?"

Sharing the work, the place is clean by noon. I tell Carol, "There are benefits to having two women in the house. Ben never did housework. Often, he put the laundry in, cooked or cleared up the table, but the rest of the work fell to me. It leaves energy and time for me to do the things I want, when someone else shares the work."

I say, "I'd like to take a University course. I know I have a Bachelor of Science already, but it seems like the right move. Even with a degree, a seventy-year-old has a slim chance of getting a regular job. The University of Washington is minutes away and seniors can audit courses for free through the Access Program. The OLLI-UW program has courses for people over fifty. That might be the right place to start. Coursera provides free courses on-line from most universities in the world. I will decide what I want to do for a future career and plan the required courses. It's scary to think about working full time and want to test if I can still study and learn. What is a suitable next step for me? In a few years I'll get back in the workforce."

With a look which suggests I might be crazy, she says, "I guess a two-year program would be best. Let's check on the web when we get back." We change for the gym and with our warm coats and scarfs, scurry to my car where Carol buckles up.

"Ya gotta love this seat heater," Carol says with a flick of the switch on the door.

CHAPTER 15

Planning a life for the NEW me:
Future bright, young and free.
Find a person whom I trust.
Friendship only, if I must.

*W*e stop by Carol's apartment to grab an overnight bag. I'm serious about researching my future career and training path but, I'm afraid, for her it is an excuse to spend time with me. I enjoy her company and living here, by myself, would be lonely. As skies darken, streetlights come on and a chill hurries us into the house.

I sit at the computer where I'm diverted to check on Russ' game schedule. He will finish early if his team doesn't make the finals. Why don't I admit my relationship with him is over? When I'm eighty, he'll be sixty-six, younger than I am now! When I think about an eighty-year-old woman being with Russ, it seems ridiculous. I will forget about him, like he's forgotten about me.

Carol brings a kitchen chair into my office. I roll to one side to share the screen. She takes a pad of lined paper and pen from the tray of supplies and writes: Interests, Opportunities, and Benefits across the top.

"What would you like your future work-space to be like?" she asks. She sounds like my life coach asking the questions. Good. Saves me a three-month contract. I smile.

"What's funny?" she asks.

"Nothing." I don't want to interrupt her process. "Work with intelligent people, not alone and a mix of physical and mental challenges." I lean back and closing my eyes, I imagine being at work." It should be indoors and we wear casual clothes. I have a degree in pharmacy, but for years I've been out of the workforce. "Frowning, I sit back up. "I'm thinking about handing out some resumes for part-time work, but not optimistic about being hired." Out in the garden, a squirrel distracts me. Carol taps her pencil and I continue. "My future can be in a science field, but perhaps in research or something state-of-the-art," I say. She writes brief notes in column one.

At several junior colleges there are two-year programs for Physical Therapist Assistant, Dental Hygienist, Radiologist, Operator of many medical machines such as Optical testing, MRI or X-ray. She lists them and the schools offering them. She fills in the columns with expected salaries, perks, etc.

"You know, this sounds exciting. Wish I could do the same thing. You're becoming much younger. I could never keep up. I never finished university like you did. I'd have to get on the getting younger program too. Wouldn't it be fun to go through school together again?" she says. I don't respond. This is the first she has approved of my rejuvenation program, let alone say she's interested in taking part. I don't want to jinx it.

"I could start with one of the fifty-plus programs or

auditing a UDub course first to see if I still remember how to study," I suggest.

"It's not your style. If you believe you can, you can do it. I believe in you. Pick something and start in January," she says.

"Can I sleep on it?" I say, not wanting to jump into anything this soon after completing my Huntsman World Game's goal. "There are a lot of options. I should plan to go to find work when I am in my late fifties again, unless I land something with my resume earlier."

Carol remains at the computer playing Candy Crush while I rustle up dinner. I ask her to set the table and fill our water glasses while I quickly check the Vintage schedule and results. Damn, I should forget about him. I'm torturing myself.

"They got into the Gold Division but in fifth seed. They lost their first match today. Tomorrow he could finish at noon," I yell from my desk. "He'll phone me when it's over. I would distract him during the games, that's all."

Carol doesn't follow all this but smiles. "Table's ready."

"This is a yummy dinner, Jeni. This hot potato salad made with cauliflower in place of potatoes — I never would have thought, but it works," Carol begins. Like a child at the beach, she dips in, fearing a cold resistance. "I've been thinking. I might do what you've done."

I can tell when I should be quiet so she can hear what it sounds like.

"This diet is tasty." Her bangs throw her wrinkled brows in shadow. "The fasting, if there are distractions to keep me from snacking — I can fast too." She pauses as she realizes an obstacle. "Affording the molecules might be an issue. Maybe giving up something else — damn it, Jeni, I want what you have. I want to go to school and be young again like you. I want the energy and drive that you have." Thoughts ripple through her mind like wind on water. "Thinking about growing younger instead of growing older opens up many possibilities."

"If you start now, in two years you will be about ten years younger. Fifty-nine and counting is our goal. I've got a head start on you; but you can get there." Excitement grows as I see my best friend joining me on this adventure. Instead of leaving her behind, she will be at my side, where she belongs. "I can help if you need it. I couldn't have done this without your support, you know." I'm lucky to have her in my life, and it will be amazing going back to school together if she's serious. Could be she is just saying this to hear how it sounds.

* * *

After dinner Carol says, "I'll settle in the guest room," and I follow with mixed emotions as she hangs things in the closet, tucks stuff from her bag in the drawer and takes her toothbrush to the bathroom. She is only staying one night, but I sense she's moving in. Ridiculous. She needed her toothbrush and pajamas.

I painted the guest room a soft rose with a row of floral wallpaper near the coved ceiling. White trim borders the paned window and doors. Gray nine-foot panel drapes hang at either side, but they are only for effect. A gray roller blackout blind keeps the light out. I refurbished the side table finds from the thrift store. Carol helps me bring the dresser up from the basement where the oil smell has gassed off. She will be comfortable here tonight.

While she finishes putting her stuff away, I think about future career paths. What if I was working nine to five? I am overwhelmed by the thought. How about working part time, three days a week? Taking courses will be a good start. I would love to learn about genetics; the way the molecules are causing me to get younger is fascinating. Or geology, the volcanic evidence found in the desert and here at Mount Rainier interests me. It isn't a career I need, only a push into taking courses. There are many opportunities opening up now since I'm not becoming an old woman.

"I talk about my future choices, but you haven't said what interests you, Carol."

She flops beside me on the floral spread. "I want us to decide together so it's something we both want," she says.

Here we go again. She is moving too fast, taking over my life. I'd better decide what I want my life to look like, and fast, before she invests in this relationship. I don't want to hurt her, but I need to have my space, my future, my choice. It's great that she's interested in reclaiming her youth, but she can do it from her own space. Can't she?

We lie there for several hours talking about one career option and laughing about another. We imagine ten likely scenarios. The suggestions comprise the two of us, doing things together.

"Let's talk in the morning," I say. "I can't decide when many of the options sound plausible, but scary."

"It won't be scary if we are looking out for one another," she says. "It will be a marvellous adventure."

"See you tomorrow," I say shutting the door to my room.

It's too early to sleep. There's an email from Harvey. I am disappointed but still curious. Should I date him? He's age appropriate, unlike Russ. I won't have to struggle to keep up if I date someone in their seventies. He knows what it's like to lose a spouse. He loves dancing, and is a good-looking man with his trimmed beard, tall slim physique and dry sense of humor. I know he's interested: hand kissing, emails. It wouldn't be difficult to develop a relationship with him. Comfortable was the word he used.

When I look at my reflection, I smile at the fit shape of my youth. The regeneration is giving me back the years I lost during Ben's illness. My cell phone sits on the bedside table with the volume turned up. It may still ring. I prop myself with the two white pillow shams, kick off my slippers and dim the bedside light. This was the bed Ben and I shared for many years. I have made it through the death of my beloved husband.

Now I've a future with choices to make. If I look towards growing old naturally, there are limited options: what on my bucket list doesn't take too much stamina or money; where will I live when I need someone to look after me?

But since I am growing younger, who do I want to become? Who do I want to be with, or do I want to live alone? Do I want a career, marriage, or children? How will I support myself if I outlive savings and pensions? How will I pay that looming medical bill? Are there talents, hobbies, or studies I want to pursue? How can I finance my future? Each of these questions brings its own flood of emotions. I have all the questions; now I need the answers. My answers, not Carol's. If I listen to my body, its reaction will be a clue to the answers.

My chest fills with pride as I picture my future. Something great is in store. I definitely don't want to live alone. The thought sends a lonely chill across my back. A life with Russ spreads warmth as the possibility flashes quickly but is gone with the silence of my cell phone, beside me. A curious blend of reactions to the possibility of a job, marriage and children: fear, excitement, and longing. I force myself to think about the money issues. All my life I've let others look after this, allowing a freedom to focus on my job and my family. The money I earned simply went into the financial pool, and there always seemed to be enough to afford a reasonable life style. Now, it's up to me! Still I don't want money to determine my decisions. I'm confident that there will be enough, or I will do what I have to do. Strangely, my body doesn't have any strong reaction to the financial choices, in spite of that damn bill. It's like Ben is telling me not to worry. He'll take care of me still.

Before I doze off, I get ready for bed, throw back the white duvet and shams and nestle into my favorite pillow. "Good night, my Darling," I say as the bedside lamp dims to black.

* * *

Last day of the Russ' tournament. *Good luck*, I think, as my mind runs backwards to the events in Utah. The spread-sheet of training choices and opportunities lies by the computer. I'm still milling them over when Carol emerges.

"Jim's Hilltop Service Station called. When they had my car on the hoist, they noticed the tires were bald. They're bringing in a set of all-weather tires. Can I hang out here until it's ready to pick up?" she asks.

"Yes." I fix us breakfast. I have to phone the accountant and discuss that bloody bill. Later.

"Can I help rake the back yard? Together it won't take us long," she says, setting out two place mats and napkins. It's nearly ten.

I can rid the yard of all those discarded dreams of the past and make room for new emerging ones. It's early to tell what they are; however, I'll be ready when they arrive.

By eleven, we head outside to repeat our leaf attack, this

time in the back around the fruit trees. Even wearing leather gloves, my fingers are freezing. "I'm glad we are getting this clean-up done. Winter is coming." I remember the warm breeze in St. George, lying by the pool and hiking in the mountains. That's why it seems cold today.

I stop Carol, who is retrieving leaves from the vegetable garden. "Leave them on the veggies. Let's clear the lawn and flower beds under the trees." Why can't I piece the puzzle together? I'm so resistant to Carol taking over and yet we are so good together.

She whisks toward the center of the yard, and soon the lawn is visible with a huge mound gathered in the middle. We fill the collapsible bin twice and empty it on the compost. I'll get out to turn it before April if this winter isn't too bad.

"Holy doodle, it's getting cold out," says Carol, pulling off her gloves and tossing them on the shelf with mine. She rubs her hands together and places them on my neck where I've removed my scarf.

"Whoa!" I scream. "I thought it was me because I've come from the desert. Let's fix some cocoa."

"I can't believe this isn't fattening." Carol wraps her hands around the steaming mug mounded with whipped cream. In minutes we have a salad thrown together, and when we sit at the counter to eat, my cocoa has cooled enough to drink. Tasks go faster with two workers.

"It is nice having you here. We work well together. Let's talk about your plan for getting younger so we can get on with career training," I say handing her half a bar — milk chocolate with mint.

"Yum, I love this, and I love being here with you too," she says.

For the entire afternoon we talk about our future, going

back to school together, deciding on how to spend our next fifty years.

"You know, Carol, doing this together will be amazing. It won't be easy keeping up this house, getting through our training, working our way back into employment. But doing it together will keep us on track." We've moved into the living room and flicked on the gas fireplace.

"I know it will be hard. But I've seen your success. You're a great role model, you know?" She pauses for a moment as if hesitant about saying her next thought. "I'm worried about the cost of the molecules. I have a big car bill right now and I live check to check."

The thought Jim's Service Station has closed interrupts our discussion, and Carol will have to wait until morning to pick up her vehicle.

"Oh wonderful, you'll stay tonight," I say and a wide grin spreads across her face.

Carol pitches in and makes life better for me. If it isn't someone else's agenda, if it is my idea she moves in here, it can work.

She watches TV while I answer some emails and check the Huntsman schedule again for the umpteenth time. Russ' team finished at eleven this morning, Pacific Time. Why didn't I hear from him? I'm not surprised, just bummed out. He must not want to see me again. Tomorrow I'll ask Carol to move in with me. It will be my choice, so I'm not pressured; at least I wouldn't be alone. It would make her happy too, I'm certain. After that, who knows? I might email Harvey to go dancing. I shut down the computer and head upstairs for a bath.

"See you in the morning, girlfriend," I say. Carol grunts, absorbed in a movie.

CHAPTER 16

Raining stops, clouds depart,
Sun spreads warmth into my heart.
Out of aging depths I climb.
Reveal my life, just in time.

Carol is fixing breakfast while I strip our beds and remake mine with fresh sheets. I'll leave the guest room sheets on the pillow and Carol can remake the bed. I throw back the drapes to reveal the peach tree branches dancing in the rain outside the window. Where is the wren? I wonder where she goes when it's winter. She'll be back in the spring when the trees are in bloom. Nothing for her to do but hunker down in her nest. With my room tidy, my hair and make-up done, the smell of bacon leads me to the kitchen. The water is boiling and two mugs with tea bags sit at the counter with cutlery and my molecules waiting.

"What a treat, to have someone fix my breakfast. Thank you, Carol," I say.

"It's the least I could do. You've been kind to me," she says.

"I stripped the beds. We can throw in a wash after we eat," I say measuring out my NMN.

"I want to order the molecules for me too." Carol sits on the stool beside me and leans on my arm.

"What's going on, Carol? You have always said you weren't interested."

"You are impulsive and quick to take advantage of opportunities. I've tried dozens of times to lose weight and get in shape, but I always screw up, get down on myself, and say this is who I am," she says not looking up.

"So?"

"I try to convince myself my appearance doesn't matter. Who am I going to impress, anyway? But I see you change, not only in appearance, but in the way you look at life. It is making you a better person. Your passion for life has returned. Your roles as a pharmacist, a wife, and a mother absorbed you. You never took time to find out who you are: a strong, independent, funny, caring and determined woman. I have been able to keep up with you in the gym — not a heavy workout, but I keep up and I'm getting more fit, more muscle. When we eat here, I enjoy it and don't come away bloated or tired. I want to eat that way too. But the molecules have caused a remarkable change. And it's easy. It's not that I want to impress anyone besides myself. I still don't want to live forever, but I want my years to be amazing like I know yours will be. I won't be able to catch up with you since you've already grown ten years younger, but I want to grow young too."

"You should read David Sinclair's book, *Health Span*, before you jump on board," I say.

"I've seen the effects, with you and Dot. It is enough for me," she says. "Show me how you order, okay?"

"Okay, after finishing the kitchen while you change your

sheets, I'll email the order site to you. There are other places to order the molecules, even from China, but I would want to get them tested here for purity. It might be worth the cost of testing because they are much cheaper. I know this website is trustworthy and the supplements are pure. Give me a holler when you're ready and I show you which jars I order," I say. Carol heads out, but stops in the living room.

"Hey Jeni, check this out. I'm glad we did the yard yesterday because there is a hell of a storm raging today." I see her kneeling on the sofa, looking out the picture window to the street in front of my house. Rain pelts diagonally and fierce winds whip the boulevard branches, ripping off the last of autumn's leaves. A jeep with windshield wipers at full speed stops across the street.

"This has got to be the biggest storm of the year. Bet we get a power outage," she says, but my eyes rivet on the green jeep and the tall man who is emerging from the driver's seat. Am I seeing things? Do I want him here so much I'm seeing him through the rain? It really is him! Tears pour down my cheeks. I grab my coat hanging on the hall hook, throw open the front door and run out in my slippers.

Seeing me, he breaks into a puddle-splashing run. I press myself against his wet leather jacket; his protective arms wrap around me. I can stand in this West Coast gale forever. I can stand with him forever. All doubts disappear. Dripping strings of my ruined bob smear my face with their icy chill. I hear someone yelling from the front porch about catching my death, but I know I'm catching my life.

"Come inside, you crazy man. I've missed you more than I can tell." I say, my slippers irretrievably soaked.

"I wanted to come straight from the plane, but I had some things to take care of before driving up," he says, locking his vehicle with a wave of the fob.

Carol is standing at the door as we do our three-legged walk up the path. "So, I gather this is Russell Vickers," she says. "I've heard so much about you."

"Russ, this is Carol. She's staying with me while her car is being fixed. I'm glad you'll have proper tires on it now Carol, with the dreadful road conditions now," I say leading my man inside. Does this sound like it's time to hit the road? It will offend her. But it's true.

"Am I in the far North? I thought the rain was a drizzle in Seattle," he says.

"It will ease up soon. It's a cold front," I say, wondering how we can chat about the weather. I want to hold him forever.

"I'll fix you some breakfast. We've finished ours, but I haven't cleaned up yet," I say. "I want to hear about Second Session and why you didn't call me."

"I will go pack my stuff and tidy up," says Carol. I can tell she's not happy, but I don't let her spoil this reunion. As much as I love Carol, as much as our friendship means to me, I have to make room for the man I love. He has to be my priority if we are going to have a successful relationship. There's friendship and there's my love for Russ. My smile is a mile wide.

Soon the marvelous smell of his breakfast fills the house. Russ settles at the counter and rests his head in his hands. He's exhausted after driving for four hours.

"I stashed my bags under the water barrel table in the gym after checking out of the Fairfield yesterday. I pushed it way back so it wouldn't get soaked by the sloppy guys overflowing their water bottles. As soon as our team lost the last match, I caught a ride to Vegas with a guy who was driving through to Los Angeles. I imagine you know we placed fourth and how we did in our games from on-line results.

An early flight to Portland got me back by dinner. It cost fifty bucks to change my flight, but it was worth it. Beth was home when I called and when I asked if she would file the divorce papers I'd filled out, she told me to come right over. I think she is sorry for the effect our split-up has had on me and wanted to move ahead with the divorce. Her partner was there when I showed up and they are happy together. I know she did the right thing — such a courageous move to leave a marriage which isn't working for you — to face ridicule from society because your lifestyle choice isn't the norm."

"I also phoned the girl I told you about to let her know I won't be seeing her again; I have fallen for someone else; and I am asking her to marry me in the morning," he says, eying me for a sign of approval. It seems crazy that he wants to marry me after such a short time, but I've wanted him in my life since we first met.

So, our life choice isn't the norm either: there is a tremendous age difference between us; we only met two weeks ago; but we are not children. We know what we want, don't we?

My mind races through all the viable life choices which have been presenting for me. Do I want to be a single lady and live alone? I would not have to answer to anyone, I could follow my dreams and interests without restriction by another's agenda. No! That's not the way for me to live. I always shared my life and would be lonely by myself. I'm flexible enough to create a life with a partner. Do I want to live with my best friend like college roommates? That would be Carol's choice. It would be a better alternative than living alone, but I'd be settling for second best. Do I want a comfortable relationship with a good old friend who is my age? Or do I want to create a loving relationship with this darling man as my husband? Yes! Yes! Yes! But I still have one question before I say yes.

"Before I give you my answer, I need to know. Why didn't you call, or text, or email, Russ? Why didn't you let me know you still love me?" I say.

"I knew I had to focus on the games. I wanted for both of us to be sure it wasn't only a Huntsman Games romance. I figured I would have no contact for the rest of the tournament. Drive straight up here and assume you want me too," he says.

"You *assumed* I wanted time to decide how I felt? You *assumed* I'd feel the same? Please — don't — *assume* you know what's best for me." I punch the words out. "I was missing you every minute and imagining terrible reasons for you not calling. Next time, let's discuss what works for both of us," I say.

"Jeez. You're right! We should have made that decision together. I'm sorry," he says. "It was clear in my mind and I was eager to get back here to ask you to marry me." He stands and wraps his arms around my trembling body.

"What? You show up in the rain after not a word since I left St. George and ask me to marry you?" I try to discipline my voice, to maintain complete control. Inside the idea germinates and my mind bulges with unasked questions. The only question that matters is this — 'Do I love Russ and want to be his wife?'

"YES!" I shout, placing my hands on his chest. "Russ, there are many details we have to work out, but when I think of life with you, it is a future in Technicolor; without you it is black and white. With you, it's three-dimensional instead of two. Working it out will be part of the adventure. I know I love you. I know you will stand with me in my choices because of the man you are. I will stand by you in your choices and I think this is your first exceptionally smart choice." I am babbling.

"We'll go pick out rings tomorrow, if you like," he says choosing breakfast over smothering me with kisses. He probably has eaten nothing until now.

"Thanks for this. I forgot to eat last night and couldn't sleep. I hit the road at four in the morning. I thought I'd stop along the way, but I was doing all right with light traffic until the weather turned. I wanted to get here before the roads became dismal. I heard about a serious accident on I-5, but I missed it by minutes." He gulps down his water.

As Russ finishes his breakfast, I run upstairs to tell Carol the news.

"We're getting married," I say as she closes her bag on the freshly made bed. The room is tidy.

"What about us? Where does this leave me?" She has been crying. "I thought we would be besties forever. We never got together when you were Ben's wife until he got sick. We've been planning how great our lives would be together. Now you have another husband who will have your attention. You won't have any time for me or for our plans. I know I won't be able to do my make-over without your help."

"I love him, Carol," I say.

"And I love you, Jeni. I always have, and I always will," she sobs. "I let myself believe that we were going to school together and have the life I've always dreamed of. I want to get in shape as you have. I need you to help me do that, Jeni."

"I love you too, Carol, as a friend. But Russ gives my life meaning. I know we will be happy; why can't you be happy for us?" I say.

"Well, I can't be happy for you, when I'm so sad for me. I

know you don't need me here — or want me here." With her bag in tow, she heads out. "I've called a cab. I'll wait outside."

"Don't be silly. I'll drive you to pick up your car."

"No, you stay here with Russ. I have to go." Wrapping her scarf and throwing up the hood on her jacket, she slams the front door.

I can't think about Carol now. If she's throwing a hissy-fit and giving up on all our plans because Russ has turned up, well, screw her. Tomorrow, I'll call her. She will have settled down by tomorrow, I hope.

I will call the kids and give them the news about Russ. Darlene is forty-six, and what does it make Gord? Forty-three this November! But they are still my kids. In the living room, I make the calls. A conference call connects both at the same time.

"Hi, how are my Darlings?" I ask, since they both pick up on the second ring.

"We're all good here, Mom." Darlene answers first.

"My better half has a cold, but otherwise, we're doing great. How are you? How was your latest trip? Utah, right?" Gord asks.

I'm buzzing with excitement. "Trip was fantastic. We won the Gold in the fifty-five division. But that's not why I called. The best part of the trip was meeting my husband. Well, we haven't married yet, but he proposed and I said 'yes'. I wanted you to know first." There was silence on the line.

Gord says, "You're joking, right? You met a guy two weeks ago and now you're engaged? Are you all right, Mom?"

"I've never been better. Russ has a house in Oregon and I will ask him to move in here with me." My voice settles with determination. "He's able to work from home."

Darlene's voice is shrill. "What? He's moving into our house? How come he's still working?"

"Hold it, kids. It's my house and my decision about who lives here. He's still working because he's only fifty-six." This will get a rise out of them.

"You're making all this up to pull our chains, right?" Gord has a hard time taking me seriously.

"I've never been this serious about anything, Gord. I have been doing an age reversal program which has turned me into a younger woman. It's more than working out and losing weight. At the volleyball tournament, I played like I was a fit sixty-year-old. I look young; I am young again; and a young man loves me. I love him. I supported you when you chose your partners, and I expect the same courtesy from you.

Darlene can't believe someone only ten years older than her would want to marry her mother. "But you're a grandmother! Maybe he's after your money, Mom. How can you be sure? What would Dad think? You're bringing a strange man into his house to sleep in his bed."

"He isn't after my money. You should see the hospital bill I got. I'll be lucky to keep the house. Besides, your father would want me to be happy. Russ makes me happy and I want you to be happy for me too. When you meet him, you'll understand. I've got to go now. Say hi to everyone on your end."

"Your grandchildren need a grandma who's there for them. Here you go again. Can't you act your age? Mom, you know we love you, but I think you are nuts," Darlene says.

"Certifiably," Gord adds.

My heart beats a mile a minute when the call disconnects. I sit alone on the sofa, grasping my cell phone while the truth registers. My own children don't want me to remarry. They think I am crazy asking a man whom I just met to come and live in their family home. Especially someone much younger than me. Is this what a grandmother would do? Hearing this from my children is an awakening experience, and it leaves me reeling. My best friend has walked out on me. How can I go through with this?

But an even more terrifying realization sweeps over me. If I do not marry Russ, I will lose the one thing that makes my life complete. I stash my phone and with fearful clarity I join my love.

In the kitchen, Russ loads the dishwasher. I don't want him to see how upset I am. With the back of my sleeve, I brush my tears away.

He turns his smile to me, "What shall we do today?"

"Bring your things in. Our room is top of the stairs," I say. He smiles, remembering our other room.

"I saw Carol getting into a cab. Is everything all right between you?" Russ sets two enormous suitcases on the entrance carpet while he hangs up his dripping jacket.

"It crushes her we're getting married. She's afraid of losing me again, like she did when I married Ben. I'll call her tomorrow and work things out." I don't want this to spoil what we have. "I have something important to discuss with you."

"What's that, Babe?" His looks troubled yet compassionate.

"I received a huge hospital bill, which I've pushed aside. I know I have to deal with it. We are a couple now, but this debt is mine. I'll take care of it, but it's leaving me on the edge. I don't want to be a burden to you. It gives me a sense of comfort that you are here. It won't be easy. My career preparation is more than an option. If I outlive my pensions or we have unexpected costs, I will have a source of income." Inadequate is not a word which describes me. I have trouble meeting his gaze.

"Jeni, let's work this through together. When my house sells, I should be able to help you pay your bills." His soothing words bring tears to my eyes.

I throw my arms around his neck. "I will call my accountant and straighten it out, right now." I pause, "Did you hear something on the porch?"

CHAPTER 17

What does it take to break my heart?
Losing a friend can tear me apart,
But losing my lover —
I'd never recover!
We're meant for each other
Right from the start.

*T*he doorbell rings. It can't be Carol coming back to apologize. She would walk right in after her secret knock, similar to most people's secret knock. You know the one — dum... ditty dum dum.... dum dum. I look at Russ and shrug. Reaching past him, I open the door. On my porch, a short angry woman clutches tight to a navy trench coat, stringy hair whipping across her make-up smeared face.

"I know he's in here. Tell him we have to talk." She looks up at the tall older lady filling the door — me!

Russ squeezes by and stares dumbfounded at the woman. "Marie, what are you doing here?"

I say, "Come in, out of the storm. You must be freezing."
This must be someone Russ knows, and she looks pathetic
huddling on my veranda. She steps forward so we can shut
the door behind her. "Russ, take her coat. I'll turn on the fireplace and bring in some tea. I'll join you in the living room."

A stranger whose eyes are puffy from crying has
appeared, cold and drenched, claiming to want my
boyfriend. Russ calls her Marie. Where does she come
from? How does she know he is here? He just arrived. This is
confusing. But if she's a friend of Russ', then she is a friend
of mine. The kettle boils. I drop some market-spice tea bags
into the mugs, and fix a tray with stevia and cream. A plate
of cut up chocolate bars complete my offering.

Russ sits beside Marie with his arm around her; she is
sobbing. I set the tray in front of them, take a fragrant mug
and settle on a nearby chair, waiting for an explanation.
None comes. I get a box of tissues to set beside the tray.
Marie pulls out a few and wipes her eyes, her nose, and her
eyes again. Immediate propane flames have warmed the
room. By turning on two lamps, I have done all I can do. I'm
getting impatient.

"What are you doing out in this storm and how do you
know Russ?" My voice is calm.

Russ shrugs with his arm still around the little blonde
with the big breasts heaving under a pink cashmere. "This is
Marie. The girl I told you about from Portland," he sighs
with exasperation.

The sudden realization shatters me. She drives four
hours to fight for the man she loves and I'm serving her tea!
Rage bubbles up, flushing my face. If she wants a fight, she
won't know what hit her. She is no match for me. I could
snap her in two. Basketball opponents would joke that my

elbows are lethally-registered weapons. But this is no joking matter. Paralysis freezes me in place. My expression hasn't changed and I sip, gripping my mug with both hands.

"You must have had a tiring drive, Marie." I try not to spit my words.

"How did you find me?" Russ seems more confused than I.

"When you hung up, I drove straight over to your place to convince you it was a mistake to give up what we have for a stranger." As a mountain lion protects her den, she hisses in my direction, "And now I can see she is much older than you too. We will have a family together. She can't give you that!" She bats damp her eyes at Russ. "But you left, so I went to Beth's."

"You went to my ex-wife's at midnight? How do you know where she lives?" His arm draws away, making a space between them.

"I know everything about you. I planned my future around you, Russ. I love you." Long lashes squeeze out another tear for effect. "Beth gave me the address you left, so I raced here."

He cares for her, and she loves him. He had his arm around her, comforting her. It amazes him she would drive four hours in a storm to fight for him.

She is right. I am too old for Russ. I'm fourteen years older than him — and infertile. Look at that sexy little body curled up on the sofa next to him. And look at me, sitting like a matron serving tea. Who am I kidding? The thought tears at my insides.

"You two have lots to talk about. I'll fix you a bowl of soup. You must have driven straight through. Bring her bag in to the guest room, because she will stay the night." I disappear to the kitchen and go through the motions of fixing a lunch for Marie. I hear her say she came without a bag — she drove straight from Beth's.

"There is soup in the kitchen." My voice sounds a little croaky. I clear my throat like the elderly often do. "I'll be upstairs in my room." There is an emphasis on 'my' and I'm sure it will register with Russ. A desperate glare of his gorgeous brown eyes follows me to the stairs.

"Let's try Jeni's soup." Russ' voice sounds calm and reassuring as he takes her hand and leads her through my house.

My bedroom closes in around me. Though only late afternoon, the darkness of this moment shutters any light from my windows. Propped by my pillows, I phone Carol.

"Hi," I say when Carol answers. "I'm sorry for treating you the way I did."

"You're sorry? You shattered my vision. You know how scared I was to let myself believe I could change. It was an enormous step for me and you smashed it. I am so hurt." She is on the verge of tears again.

"I think you're afraid," I say. "You helped me when I was down, but it became a distraction for you. You ignored your own situation. Now you don't know how to ease up. You are afraid you can't reinvent yourself alone."

"You got that last part right." Carol's voice breaks.

"Okay, get it together. It's my turn. Listen. You're going to wanta hear this! Russ' girlfriend from Portland showed up. They're in the kitchen having soup right now!" Telling Carol eases some pain. "She's in her early forties. She's telling me how much she loves him and that she knows everything about him. I know nothing about him — except I love him. She wants to have his kids, and I can't do that either. Carol, I'm afraid I have to lose him."

Will she try to encourage me to send him away so we can

pick up where we were yesterday? He only showed up this morning and my life has been like a roller coaster ever since. As I am settling for a life with Carol, Russ turns up. I am ecstatic but angry because he assumed what I wanted and didn't call. I offended my buddy and sent her home. Marie stealing the man I love threatens the bliss of our short time together. The branch whips against the window above my head as the storm continues to rage outside and in.

"I'm sorry," my friend sympathies. "What does Russell say?"

"Nothing. He's said nothing. I'm putting her up in the guest room. He'll sleep on the sofa until they can work it out. I will not sleep with him, knowing that she is seething in the next room. And perhaps he wants to sleep in there with her. Carol, my heart is breaking." The controlled exterior melts as my eyes fill; tears slip down my cheeks.

"Call me later when you get settled. I want all the juicy details — all of them. We'll get through this. We always do." When the phone goes dead, I am alone again sitting in the dark.

Remembering the other call, I dial my accountant. "Yes, you have hundreds of thousands in your investments, but now is not the time to take it out. October is volatile. Perhaps we should look into some other option — a reverse mortgage, perhaps? When you pass away, we pay the debt off from the equity in the house."

"No, that isn't an option. Take the money out of the investments. I can live on my pensions until I can get back into the work force," I say, thinking out loud.

"What do you mean, in the work force? You've got to be joking, right?" he says.

"Never mind. See that this bill gets paid. I'm emailing a copy to you today." I wish him a good day.

I creep down to join the couple in the kitchen. Interrupting them is not my intent. I listen for an intimate conversation. Instead, I hear Russ' angry tones.

"I'm pissed that you don't take me at my word. When I say I won't be seeing you anymore, I mean it. I love her. We are getting married. You don't belong here in her house. There is nothing between us anymore — not even respect, if you drive all this way to defy me."

Her voice is emphatic, but softer. "How can you marry someone fourteen years older than you? What kind of life, taking care of an elderly woman?" I listen, riveted and seething on the stair.

"So how old are you, Marie? Fourteen years younger than me! What difference do ages make, anyway? She is more fit and stronger than you. And I don't have the same problem in bed that I had with you," he says, pulling out the trump card.

She is silent. I step down onto the squeaky step, announcing my approach. "Marie, I want you to have our guest room for the night. Russ, I'll put bedding out on the sofa. That's best until you two work this out," I state. "I'll loan you a tee shirt to sleep in. Would you like to bathe before you go to bed? The bathroom in the upstairs hall is for guests. You'll find a hair dryer and everything you might need." Except Russ. This is a hint that she should get out of my sight while I am still civil.

"I called Carol while I was upstairs. That drama's calm now. I'll be right back." Marie grabs for her purse on the way and follows me. With a toss, my Huntsman Games tee shirt lands on the guest bed. I open the door to the bathroom. "Breakfast is at eight. Don't be late." I sound cheerful while inside the tumult churns.

Down in the kitchen, Russ looks exhausted — head

resting on his arms, supported by the counter. From the stool facing, I swing him to look at me. "What do you want? That's all that is important. It's the rest of your life we're talking about." I need to cling to him yet realize the choice is his.

"I'm sleeping on the sofa? I'm six foot five!" He sulks. His arms slump on my shoulders and our foreheads touch. "You know, I only want a life with you. Marie coming up here doesn't change that for a minute."

"I'm sure you can curl up on the sofa. You're so tired that you could even sleep on the rug. Your choice. Shower in my bathroom while I fix some quilts and pillows for you. There is some fruit and cheese in case you get hungry." Scurrying into these tasks, I leave Russ to slink dejected up the stairs.

A towel conceals his lower half as he returns. He gets a quick peck goodnight as he bundles beneath the blankets. Like a toddler being tucked in, he asks for a glass of water. I slap him on the shoulder and say, "Get it yourself. You live here now."

He smiles and within minutes, he's asleep.

* * *

"Carol, did I wake you?" This is my first opportunity to call.

"Not asleep yet. How's it hanging?" She seems in better spirits.

"Marie is in the guest room, and Russ is asleep in the living room. I'm like a warden punishing him for her appearance. It will work out. He'll send her packing in the morning. She's sleeping in my Huntsman tee shirt but won't see the irony of it."

"You're bad — in a good way. But you don't know for sure, right?" she says.

"Ninety percent sure — wait, someone is opening my door. Gotta go. I'll call tomorrow." A hand reaches in and gropes for the light switch. The room goes black. A tall figure creeps to the far side of the bed and slides under the duvet. Trembling, my heart in my throat, I set my phone onto the bedside table and crawl in on the other side.

At seven, the sun shines in above the bed, waking us both. Nodding my head toward the bathroom and swinging my legs free of the covers, I'm up for the day. The shower is soothing until I finish with a minute of chilly water. It was difficult at first, but now I end every shower with it cranked to the left. Russ dresses while I hurry down to make breakfast, a towel-wrapped head matching my terry bathrobe. Marie should see what Russ is choosing. I fix our usual fat-infused high protein breakfast, adding a bed of extra cooked onions, peppers and mushrooms beneath the scrambled eggs with salsa and guacamole. The smell of the bacon and onions brings both Russ and Marie downstairs. She looks at the rumpled quilts in the living room and then at Russell, who gives no hint he spent the night upstairs.

"You need a big breakfast before you hit the road, Marie." My voice is saying, but I'm meaning, "I'm not sorry you didn't get what you came for. Too bad — you lose!"

I carry on as though she isn't even sitting with us. "We should talk about Carol before I call her this morning. She's calming down and I'm wondering if we still want her to come live with us."

He picks up on the thread that Marie's presence has no impact on our relationship, which will weather all intrusions. He answers me. "This sends up warning signs for me, you know. Having gone through a break-up caused by two women who fell in love, I have to admit I'm concerned. She loves you, Jeni." The shadow of his beard gives his concerned face a manlier aura. I try concentrating on his words, ignoring the warmth spreading through me and the bitch sitting next to him.

"I know, and I love her. We have been best friends since high school. She had a dysfunctional home life. She sees me as family. I'm not attracted to her, and she has never shown me she wants involvement that way. She wants to change the way I have, but is afraid to do it on her own. I want to support her as much as she has supported me. She and I plan to take courses preparing for our future careers. She wants to rejuvenate. If it hadn't been for her, I wouldn't have gone to the Huntsman Games and I would not have met you. I owe her so much."

"Where are you going with this?"

"I want Carol to stay here, as a boarder. That way she can save the money she needs for the supplements. I can help her with all of it. I know she won't do it without my support. It's too hard to stay on track without a sympathetic support system. That has to be me," I say.

"That explains her disappearance yesterday? She figures the entire plan is being scrapped," he says.

Having great peripheral vision, I can see without turning my head, this conversation mesmerizes Marie. She expects to be the focal point, and now she is an intruder amid a personal discussion which doesn't even register her existence.

"Thanks for breakfast, Jeni. I still think you made the wrong choice, Russ, but it's time to lick my wounds and head back home. You know the song, 'don't you ever for a second get to thinking, you're irreplaceable'."

"Good luck, Marie," he says. "Sorry you made the drive for nothing. I only say what I mean. You should have listened."

"You're right. That's one thing I love about you. But I couldn't give up without trying." She slings her trench coat over her arm and heads to her car, oblivious of the morning chill. We can't see her cry, because she doesn't look back.

CHAPTER 18

I become an academic,
Thriving through the dread pandemic.
Overcoming all, it seems;
Growing young with love and dreams.

*R*uss' bags sit in the foyer. We carry one each up the stairs to our room where he pulls me towards him. A tingle of anticipation runs through me as my body presses against his. A warm glow flows through me. His kiss is gentle. He raises his mouth from mine and gazes into my eyes. Placing my hand behind his head, I pull him in and kiss him with a hunger that has been a week forming. I step out of his encircling arms and pull up his sweater. He needs no more encouragement than that.

He flips the covers to reveal the welcoming sheets still rumpled from our sleep together. Naked, Russ climbs in, moving to the far side. Our clothes heap together while I join him, my breasts brushing the hair on his chest. His muscular arm flops over my waist. I sense calm, protection, completeness. Russ is asleep.

He wakes me by turning over. I spoon against him as my arm tucks around his middle and the rest of me curls into the curve of his body. His loving hand covers mine and squeezes. He moves my hand lower, urging it to explore. It rests on his erection. Excitement blossoms and when I grip it, his tormented groan is a heady invitation. I roll him onto his back and mount him. He reaches to caress my taunting breasts and the loving brush of his fingers on my skin hardens my nipples while he extends deep inside me. There is no urgency or expectation. The tempo we find binds our bodies together as we drift toward a climax. Waves of ecstasy pulse through me and his love flows into me like warm honey. My body melts against his, heaving sighs of pleasant exhaustion.

"Join me for another shower?" I say minutes later as I slip out of bed. While the water rinses away the sleep and sex from my body, Russ steps in behind me to caress and explore with sudsy hands. I turn, allowing the full force of the shower to hit him. He seems to enjoy being washed so I can't say the pleasure is all mine.

"You hungry?" I ask as we are drying off.

"What cha got?" he asks. "A roundabout way of saying "yes".

"I'll find something," I say, pulling on my bathrobe.

* * *

"What you said earlier about living here with me, sounds good. I was hoping you would want that. I talked to my accountant and have paid the hospital bill, which doesn't leave me with a lot of investment income. After we marry, we can decide if we want to stay here or get a place of our own somewhere. You said you are selling your house in Oregon?" I take our dishes off the counter.

"Yes, I've listed it."

"Jeni, I've given it a lot of thought — what we talked about in front of Marie." He pauses, making me think he's changed his mind, "I think it will be fun having Carol here. You'll have help with keeping the place up, the money will lessen house expenses, and it will give you company when I'm working. Let's do it!"

I throw my arms around him. "Thanks for agreeing to this. It looks like all my dreams are coming true — and Carol's too."

"This house is roomy enough. Carol can rent some space. Your plans of going to classes together could be a reality, providing there is only friendship involved — I'm not into threesomes either." Russ grins at the thought.

"I'm calling her. Put your things away? There are empty drawers and half the closet waiting for you." I've kept a huge empty spot in my heart, there for you.

Dozens of naked hangers wait on the rack across from my clothes. I've always been on the right, Ben on the left. Only a sweater and bomber jacket hang at one end. Russ hesitates.

"It's okay. I only kept a few things. We can hang them next to my skirts if they bother you." I say, understanding it is difficult for him to not only move into Ben's house, sleep with his wife, and now have to share a closet with his clothes. I push back my hangers to make room and slip them at the end.

"They're too small for me," Russ says, "but you might enjoy wearing them, or saving them for your son."

"That's a wonderful idea. Gord lives in Australia. He would love that. There might be some other things to send to Darlene. I'll get on with that call." I leave Russ and check out the guest room while I dial. At least Marie left the room tidy. She stripped the bed, but left it easy to remake with fresh sheets. A shudder spreads through me, realizing how close I was to the precipice. Russ returning with Marie to Oregon would shatter me. Instead, I enjoy the warm calm of him loving me from the next room. I would still have had Carol. I'll always have her in my life.

"You helped me beyond what I can repay." I tell Carol as soon as I reach her. "We want you to come and live here, help us with our wedding. I'll support you with regeneration and some lifestyle changes. We'll still plan our careers and take courses, but they may be on separate paths. You can pay rent and board, help with the chores, and accept that my life will focus around Russ. Does that interest you?"

A silence hangs on the other end. "Did I hear you right? You still want me to come and stay with you? You will help me with my makeover? We can still go to school together? You're not joking, are you? I couldn't bear if you were saying this to cheer me and not mean it."

I laugh, "No, we're not kidding. We want you for our roommate. The only stipulation is you keep your hands off Russ. He has a history of his ex-wife finding a girlfriend and leaving him, so keep your hands off me too." Considering sex with a woman seems foreign.

"If you guys mean it, I'm in. Seriously? I can't imagine how life could be more perfect!" Carol bounces with excitement. "Maybe when I get my shit together, I'll meet someone as great as Russ."

"Wait until I tell him you said that. You give notice and start packing." I want her to know we won't change our minds. With a grip on the rail, I bound downstairs, two at a time, to share the news.

I've recovered from the years that aged me through Ben's illness and restored the passions of my youth. This is as good as it gets. I will get younger with my two favorite people. Our adventures together will be legendary. We can do anything, if we have each other. This is better than being an independent woman on my own — better than sharing a life with a roommate — better than living with my life revolving around a man. I will have it all and remain fit, as long as I continue to do a few simple things.

Russ searches the fridge with his back to me as I rush in, my face flushed with excitement. "Carol is giving notice and moving in with us. There is no time to change your mind," I say.

"We haven't needed time for any of our major decisions." He turns and stares at me with his irresistible grin, which converts to laughter. "I knew when we met that I wanted to be with you. I think it will be fine to share a home with your friend. We'll show her a functional family. Carol gets the guest room for now. Could be we'll need it for a nursery next."

A nursery. He knows we will turn back the clock and our lives today prepare for our future — a future where we will need a nursery? I can't tell if he's serious when he says this, but it makes me smile.

DEAR READER

I hope you enjoyed Jeni's transition from an aging widow in Seattle to a vibrant attractive athlete competing in the Huntsman World Senior Games. When she discovered an alternative to growing older, amazing things happened. I hope you have a girlfriend as loyal as Carol and a love as genuine as Russ'.

Reviews are important to writers, offering support and reinforcing strengths. Let me know if Jeni's journey has changed yours.

* * *

Review *YOUNG — In the Age of Champions* on...

Amazon
www.amazon.ca/dp/B08JRDX1R4
www.amazon.com/dp/B08JRDX1R4

Goodreads
www.goodreads.com/book/show/55528857-young

* * *

Keep reading to see what joy and heartache fills the rest of the *TIMELESS TRILOGY*.

ALSO BY DENELDA BENDSEN

TIMELESS TRILOGY

Book One - YOUNG - In the Age of Champions
(Available Oct. 1, 2020)

Book Two - YOUNGER - In the Age of COVID
(Available Nov. 1, 2020)

Book Three - YOUNGEST - In the Age of Dreams
(Available Dec. 1, 2020)

ABOUT THE AUTHOR

Denelda Mary Bendsen is an athlete and a writer. Playing basketball for Team Canada for seven years as a young woman, she continues meddling (and medaling) in team sport into her seventies. She and her husband are growing younger with a healthy lifestyle in community on Vancouver Island. To find out more about Denelda, you can visit her website.

www.denelda.bendsens.com

www.amazon.com/DENELDA-BENDSEN/e/B08JX42CZP

www.goodreads.com/DeneldaBendsen

www.facebook.com/Denelda.Bendsens

www.instagram.com/denelda_bendsen

Made in the USA
Monee, IL
26 October 2020

46109903R00105